The Ordeal Of Richard Feverel

Volume 5

by

George Meredith

Double9 BOOKS

The Ordeal Of Richard Feverel

Volume 5

by George Meredith

ISBN: 978-93-74835-95-1

Published by

DOUBLE 9 BOOKS

2/13-B, Ansari Road
Daryaganj, New Delhi – 110002
info@double9books.com
www.double9books.com
Tel. 011-40042856

ABOUT THE AUTHOR

George Meredith was an English novelist and poet, born on February 12, 1828. Meredith was born to Thomas Meredith and Jane Cholmeley. He was a prominent figure in the Victorian era, initially known for his poetry, which was heavily influenced by poets like John Keats. Over time, Meredith transitioned into novel writing and became recognized for his works in this genre. His novel The Ordeal of Richard Feverel (1859) caused a stir in Victorian literary circles due to its controversial themes. However, it was his later novels, such as The Egoist (1879) and Diana of the Crossways (1885) that earned him enduring acclaim. His works often explored complex psychological and moral dilemmas, blending wit with serious social critique. Meredith's other notable works include The Shaving of Shagpat (1856), Farina (1857), and Evan Harrington (1861). Throughout his career, he developed a reputation for his intricate character studies and exploration of human nature. Meredith's influence extended well into the 20th century, and his work remains a key part of Victorian literature.

CONTENTS

BOOK 5

CHAPTER XXXIV 7

CHAPTER XXXV 25

CHAPTER XXXVI 37

CHAPTER XXXVII 51

CHAPTER XXXVIII 61

BOOK 5

CHAPTER XXXIV

It was the month of July. The Solent ran up green waves before a full-blowing South-wester. Gay little yachts bounded out like foam, and flashed their sails, light as sea-nymphs. A crown of deep Summer blue topped the flying mountains of cloud.

By an open window that looked on the brine through nodding roses, our young bridal pair were at breakfast, regaling worthily, both of them. Had the Scientific Humanist observed them, he could not have contested the fact, that as a couple who had set up to be father and mother of Britons, they were doing their duty. Files of egg-cups with disintegrated shells bore witness to it, and they were still at work, hardly talking from rapidity of exercise. Both were dressed for an expedition. She had her bonnet on, and he his yachting-hat. His sleeves were turned over at the wrists, and her gown showed its lining on her lap. At times a chance word might spring a laugh, but eating was the business of the hour, as I would have you to know it always will be where Cupid is in earnest. Tribute flowed in to them from the subject land. Neglected lies Love's penny-whistle on which they played so prettily and charmed the spheres to hear them. What do they care for the spheres, who have one another? Come, eggs! come, bread and butter! come, tea with sugar in it and milk! and welcome, the jolly hours. That is a fair interpretation of the music in them just now. Yonder instrument was good only for the overture. After all, what finer aspiration can lovers have, than to be free man and woman in the heart of plenty? And is it not a glorious level to have attained? Ah, wretched Scientific Humanist! not to be by and mark the admirable sight of these young creatures feeding. It would have been a spell to exorcise the Manichee, methinks.

The mighty performance came to an end, and then, with a flourish of his table-napkin, husband stood over wife, who met him on the confident budding of her mouth. The poetry of mortals is their daily prose. Is it not a glorious level to have attained? A short, quick-blooded kiss, radiant, fresh, and honest as Aurora, and then Richard says without lack of cheer,

"No letter to-day, my Lucy!" whereat her sweet eyes dwell on him a little seriously, but he cries, "Never mind! he'll be coming down himself some morning. He has only to know her, and all's well! eh?" and so saying he puts a hand beneath her chin, and seems to frame her fair face in fancy, she smiling up to be looked at.

"But one thing I do want to ask my darling," says Lucy, and dropped into his bosom with hands of petition. "Take me on board his yacht with him to-day—not leave me with those people! Will he? I'm a good sailor, he knows!"

"The best afloat!" laughs Richard, hugging her, "but, you know, you darling bit of a sailor, they don't allow more than a certain number on board for the race, and if they hear you've been with me, there'll be cries of foul play! Besides, there's Lady Judith to talk to you about Austin, and Lord Mountfalcon's compliments for you to listen to, and Mr. Morton to take care of you."

Lucy's eyes fixed sideways an instant.

"I hope I don't frown and blush as I did?" she said, screwing her pliable brows up to him winningly, and he bent his cheek against hers, and murmured something delicious.

"And we shall be separated for—how many hours? one, two, three hours!" she pouted to his flatteries.

"And then I shall come on board to receive my bride's congratulations."

"And then my husband will talk all the time to Lady Judith."

"And then I shall see my wife frowning and blushing at Lord Mountfalcon."

"Am I so foolish, Richard?" she forgot her trifling to ask in an earnest way, and had another Aurorean kiss, just brushing the dew on her lips, for answer.

After hiding a month in shyest shade, the pair of happy sinners had wandered forth one day to look on men and marvel at them, and had chanced to meet Mr. Morton of Poer Hall, Austin Wentworth's friend, and Ralph's uncle. Mr. Morton had once been intimate with the baronet, but had given him up for many years as impracticable and hopeless, for which reason he was the more inclined to regard Richard's misdemeanour charitably, and to lay the faults of the son on the father; and thinking society to be the one thing requisite to the young man, he had introduced him to the people he knew in the island; among others to the Lady Judith Felle, a fair young dame, who introduced him to Lord Mountfalcon, a puissant nobleman; who introduced him to the yachtsmen beginning to congregate;

so that in a few weeks he found himself in the centre of a brilliant company, and for the first time in his life tasted what it was to have free intercourse with his fellow-creatures of both sews. The son of a System was, therefore, launched; not only through the surf, but in deep waters.

Now the baronet had so far compromised between the recurrence of his softer feelings and the suggestions of his new familiar, that he had determined to act toward Richard with justness. The world called it magnanimity, and even Lady Blandish had some thoughts of the same kind when she heard that he had decreed to Richard a handsome allowance, and had scouted Mrs. Doria's proposal for him to contest the legality of the marriage; but Sir Austin knew well he was simply just in not withholding money from a youth so situated. And here again the world deceived him by embellishing his conduct. For what is it to be just to whom we love! He knew it was not magnanimous, but the cry of the world somehow fortified him in the conceit that in dealing perfect justice to his son he was doing all that was possible, because so much more than common fathers would have done. He had shut his heart.

Consequently Richard did not want money. What he wanted more, and did not get, was a word from his father, and though he said nothing to sadden his young bride, she felt how much it preyed upon him to be at variance with the man whom, now that he had offended him and gone against him, he would have fallen on his knees to; the man who was as no other man to him. She heard him of nights when she lay by his side, and the darkness, and the broken mutterings, of those nights clothed the figure of the strange stern man in her mind. Not that it affected the appetites of the pretty pair. We must not expect that of Cupid enthroned and in condition; under the influence of sea-air, too. The files of egg-cups laugh at such an idea. Still the worm did gnaw them. Judge, then, of their delight when, on this pleasant morning, as they were issuing from the garden of their cottage to go down to the sea, they caught sight of Tom Bakewell rushing up the road with a portmanteau on his shoulders, and, some distance behind him, discerned Adrian.

"It's all right!" shouted Richard, and ran off to meet him, and never left his hand till he had hauled him up, firing questions at him all the way, to where Lucy stood.

"Lucy! this is Adrian, my cousin."—"Isn't he an angel?" his eyes seemed to add; while Lucy's clearly answered, "That he is!"

The full-bodied angel ceremoniously bowed to her, and acted with reserved unction the benefactor he saw in their greetings. "I think we are not strangers," he was good enough to remark, and very quickly let them know he had not breakfasted; on hearing which they hurried him into the house, and Lucy put herself in motion to have him served.

"Dear old Rady," said Richard, tugging at his hand again, "how glad I am you've come! I don't mind telling you we've been horridly wretched."

"Six, seven, eight, nine eggs," was Adrian's comment on a survey of the breakfast-table.

"Why wouldn't he write? Why didn't he answer one of my letters? But here you are, so I don't mind now. He wants to see us, does he? We'll go up to-night. I've a match on at eleven; my little yacht—I've called her the 'Blandish'—against Fred Cuirie's 'Begum.' I shall beat, but whether I do or not, we'll go up to-night. What's the news? What are they all doing?"

"My dear boy!" Adrian returned, sitting comfortably down, "let me put myself a little more on an equal footing with you before I undertake to reply. Half that number of eggs will be sufficient for an unmarried man, and then we'll talk. They're all very well, as well as I can recollect after the shaking my total vacuity has had this morning. I came over by the first boat, and the sea, the sea has made me love mother earth, and desire of her fruits."

Richard fretted restlessly opposite his cool relative.

"Adrian! what did he say when he heard of it? I want to know exactly what words he said."

> "Well says the sage, my son! 'Speech is the small change
> of Silence.'
> He said less than I do."

"That's how he took it!" cried Richard, and plunged in meditation.

Soon the table was cleared, and laid out afresh, and Lucy preceded the maid bearing eggs on the tray, and sat down unbonneted, and like a thorough-bred housewife, to pour out the tea for him.

"Now we'll commence," said Adrian, tapping his egg with meditative cheerfulness; but his expression soon changed to one of pain, all the more alarming for his benevolent efforts to conceal it. Could it be possible the egg was bad? oh, horror! Lucy watched him, and waited in trepidation.

"This egg has boiled three minutes and three-quarters," he observed, ceasing to contemplate it.

> "Dear, dear!" said Lucy, "I boiled them myself exactly
> that time.
> Richard likes them so. And you like them hard, Mr.
> Harley?"

"On the contrary, I like them soft. Two minutes and a half, or three-quarters at the outside. An egg should never rashly verge upon hardness--never. Three minutes is the excess of temerity."

"If Richard had told me! If I had only known!" the lovely little hostess interjected ruefully, biting her lip.

"We mustn't expect him to pay attention to such matters," said Adrian, trying to smile.

"Hang it! there are more eggs in the house," cried Richard, and pulled savagely at the bell.

Lucy jumped up, saying, "Oh, yes! I will go and boil some exactly the time you like. Pray let me go, Mr. Harley."

Adrian restrained her departure with a motion of his hand. "No," he said, "I will be ruled by Richard's tastes, and heaven grant me his digestion!"

Lucy threw a sad look at Richard, who stretched on a sofa, and left the burden of the entertainment entirely to her. The eggs were a melancholy beginning, but her ardour to please Adrian would not be damped, and she deeply admired his resignation. If she failed in pleasing this glorious herald of peace, no matter by what small misadventure, she apprehended calamity; so there sat this fair dove with brows at work above her serious smiling blue eyes, covertly studying every aspect of the plump- faced epicure, that she might learn to propitiate him. "He shall not think me timid and stupid," thought this brave girl, and indeed Adrian was astonished to find that she could both chat and be useful, as well as look ornamental. When he had finished one egg, behold, two fresh ones came in, boiled according to his prescription. She had quietly given her orders to the maid, and he had them without fuss. Possibly his look of dismay at the offending eggs had not been altogether involuntary, and her woman's instinct, inexperienced as she was, may have told her that he had come prepared to be not very well satisfied with anything in Love's cottage. There was mental faculty in those pliable brows to see through, and combat, an unwitting wise youth.

How much she had achieved already she partly divined when Adrian said: "I think now I'm in case to answer your questions, my dear boy—thanks to Mrs. Richard," and he bowed to her his first direct acknowledgment of her position. Lucy thrilled with pleasure.

"Ah!" cried Richard, and settled easily on his back.

"To begin, the Pilgrim has lost his Note-book, and has been persuaded to offer a reward which shall maintain the happy finder thereof in an asylum for life. Benson—superlative Benson—has turned his shoulders upon Raynham. None know whither he has departed. It is believed that the sole surviving member of the sect of the Shaddock-Dogmatists is under a total eclipse of Woman."

"Benson gone?" Richard exclaimed. "What a tremendous time it seems since I left Raynham!"

"So it is, my dear boy. The honeymoon is Mahomet's minute; or say, the Persian King's water-pail that you read of in the story: You dip your head in it, and when you draw it out, you discover that you have lived a life. To resume your uncle Algernon still roams in pursuit of the lost one—I should say, hops. Your uncle Hippias has a new and most perplexing symptom; a determination of bride-cake to the nose. Ever since your generous present to him, though he declares he never consumed a morsel of it, he has been under the distressing illusion that his nose is enormous, and I assure you he exhibits quite a maidenly timidity in following it—through a doorway, for instance. He complains of its terrible weight. I have conceived that Benson invisible might be sitting on it. His hand, and the doctor's, are in hourly consultation with it, but I fear it will not grow smaller. The Pilgrim has begotten upon it a new Aphorism: that Size is a matter of opinion."

"Poor uncle Hippy!" said Richard, "I wonder he doesn't believe in magic. There's nothing supernatural to rival the wonderful sensations he does believe in. Good God! fancy coming to that!"

"I'm sure I'm very sorry," Lucy protested, "but I can't help laughing."

Charming to the wise youth her pretty laughter sounded.

"The Pilgrim has your notion, Richard. Whom does he not forestall? 'Confirmed dyspepsia is the apparatus of illusions,' and he accuses the Ages that put faith in sorcery, of universal indigestion, which may have been the case, owing to their infamous cookery. He says again, if you remember, that our own Age is travelling back to darkness and ignorance through dyspepsia. He lays the seat of wisdom in the centre of our system, Mrs. Richard: for which reason you will understand how sensible I am of the vast obligation I am under to you at the present moment, for your especial care of mine."

Richard looked on at Lucy's little triumph, attributing Adrian's subjugation to her beauty and sweetness. She had latterly received a great many compliments on that score, which she did not care to hear, and Adrian's homage to a practical quality was far pleasanter to the young wife, who shrewdly guessed that her beauty would not help her much in the struggle she had now to maintain. Adrian continuing to lecture on the excelling virtues of wise cookery, a thought struck her: Where, where had she tossed Mrs. Berry's book?

"So that's all about the home-people?" said Richard.

"All!" replied Adrian. "Or stay: you know Clare's going
to be married?
Not? Your Aunt Helen" —

"Oh, bother my Aunt Helen! What do you think she had the impertinence to write—but never mind! Is it to Ralph?"

"Your Aunt Helen, I was going to say, my dear boy, is an extraordinary woman. It was from her originally that the Pilgrim first learnt to call the female the practical animal. He studies us all, you know. The Pilgrim's Scrip is the abstract portraiture of his surrounding relatives. Well, your Aunt Helen" —

"Mrs. Doria Battledoria!" laughed Richard.

"—being foiled in a little pet scheme of her own—call it a System if you like—of some ten or fifteen years' standing, with regard to Miss Clare!" —

The fair Shuttlecockiana!"

"—instead of fretting like a man, and questioning Providence, and turning herself and everybody else inside out, and seeing the world upside down, what does the practical animal do? She wanted to marry her to somebody she couldn't marry her to, so she resolved instantly to marry her to somebody she could marry her to: and as old gentlemen enter into these transactions with the practical animal the most readily, she fixed upon an old gentleman; an unmarried old gentleman, a rich old gentleman, and now a captive old gentleman. The ceremony takes place in about a week from the present time. No doubt you will receive your invitation in a day or two."

"And that cold, icy, wretched Clare has consented to marry an old man!" groaned Richard. "I'll put a stop to that when I go to town."

Richard got up and strode about the room. Then he bethought him it was time to go on board and make preparations.

"I'm off," he said. "Adrian, you'll take her. She goes in the Empress, Mountfalcon's vessel. He starts us. A little schooner-yacht—such a beauty! I'll have one like her some day. Good-bye, darling!" he whispered to Lucy, and his hand and eyes lingered on her, and hers on him, seeking to make up for the priceless kiss they were debarred from. But she quickly looked away from him as he held her:—Adrian stood silent: his brows were up, and his mouth dubiously contracted. He spoke at last.

"Go on the water?"

"Yes. It's only to St. Helen's. Short and sharp."

"Do you grudge me the nourishment my poor system has just received, my son?"

"Oh, bother your system! Put on your hat, and come along. I'll put you on board in my boat."

"Richard! I have already paid the penalty of them who are condemned to come to an island. I will go with you to the edge of the sea, and I will meet you there when you return, and take up the Tale of the Tritons: but, though I forfeit the pleasure of Mrs. Richard's company, I refuse to quit the land."

"Yes, oh, Mr. Harley!" Lucy broke from her husband, "and I will stay with you, if you please. I don't want to go among those people, and we can see it all from the shore.

"Dearest! I don't want to go. You don't mind? Of course, I will go if you wish, but I would so much rather stay;" and she lengthened her plea in her attitude and look to melt the discontent she saw gathering.

Adrian protested that she had much better go; that he could amuse himself very well till their return, and so forth; but she had schemes in her pretty head, and held to it to be allowed to stay in spite of Lord Mountfalcon's disappointment, cited by Richard, and at the great risk of vexing her darling, as she saw. Richard pished, and glanced contemptuously at Adrian. He gave way ungraciously.

"There, do as you like. Get your things ready to leave this evening. No, I'm not angry."—Who could be? he seemed as he looked up from her modest fondling to ask Adrian, and seized the indemnity of a kiss on her forehead, which, however, did not immediately disperse the shade of annoyance he felt.

"Good heavens!" he exclaimed. "Such a day as this, and a fellow refuses to come on the water! Well, come along to the edge of the sea." Adrian's angelic quality had quite worn off to him. He never thought of devoting himself to make the most of the material there was: but somebody else did, and that fair somebody succeeded wonderfully in a few short hours. She induced Adrian to reflect that the baronet had only to see her, and the family muddle would be smoothed at once. He came to it by degrees; still the gradations were rapid. Her manner he liked; she was certainly a nice picture: best of all, she was sensible. He forgot the farmer's niece in her, she was so very sensible. She appeared really to understand that it was a woman's duty to know how to cook.

But the difficulty was, by what means the baronet could be brought to consent to see her. He had not yet consented to see his son, and Adrian, spurred by Lady Blandish, had ventured something in coming down. He was not inclined to venture more. The small debate in his mind ended by his throwing the burden on time. Time would bring the matter about. Christians as well as Pagans are in the habit of phrasing this excuse for folding their arms; "forgetful," says The Pilgrim's Scrip, "that the devil's imps enter into no such armistice."

As she loitered along the shore with her amusing companion, Lucy had many things to think of. There was her darling's match. The yachts were started by pistol-shot by Lord Mountfalcon on board the Empress, and her little heart beat after Richard's straining sails. Then there was the strangeness of walking with a relative of Richard's, one who had lived by his side so long. And the thought that perhaps this night she would have to appear before the dreaded father of her husband.

"O Mr. Harley!" she said, "is it true—are we to go tonight? And me," she faltered, "will he see me?"

"Ah! that is what I wanted to talk to you about," said Adrian. "I made some reply to our dear boy which he has slightly misinterpreted. Our second person plural is liable to misconstruction by an ardent mind. I said 'see you,' and he supposed—now, Mrs. Richard, I am sure you will understand me. Just at present perhaps it would be advisable—when the father and son have settled their accounts, the daughter-in-law can't be a debtor."...

Lucy threw up her blue eyes. A half-cowardly delight at the chance of a respite from the awful interview made her quickly apprehensive.

"O Mr. Harley! you think he should go alone first?"

"Well, that is my notion. But the fact is, he is such an excellent husband that I fancy it will require more than a man's power of persuasion to get him to go."

"But I will persuade him, Mr. Harley."

"Perhaps, if you would..."

"There is nothing I would not do for his happiness," murmured Lucy.

The wise youth pressed her hand with lymphatic approbation. They walked on till the yachts had rounded the point.

"Is it to-night, Mr. Harley?" she asked with some trouble in her voice now that her darling was out of sight.

"I don't imagine your eloquence even will get him to leave you to-night," Adrian replied gallantly. "Besides, I must speak for myself. To achieve the passage to an island is enough for one day. No necessity exists for any hurry, except in the brain of that impetuous boy. You must correct it, Mrs. Richard. Men are made to be managed, and women are born managers. Now, if you were to let him know that you don't want to go to- night, and let him guess, after a day or two, that you would very much rather... you might affect a peculiar repugnance. By taking it on yourself, you see, this wild young man will not require such frightful efforts of persuasion. Both his father and he are exceedingly delicate subjects, and his father unfortunately is not in a position to be managed directly. It's a strange office to propose to you, but it appears to devolve upon you to manage the father through the son. Prodigal having made his peace, you, who have done all the work from a distance, naturally come into the circle of the paternal smile, knowing it due to you. I see no other way. If Richard suspects that his father objects for the present to welcome his daughter-in-law, hostilities will be continued, the breach will be widened, bad will grow to worse, and I see no end to it."

Adrian looked in her face, as much as to say: Now are you capable of this piece of heroism? And it did seem hard to her that she should have to tell Richard she shrank from any trial. But the proposition chimed in with her fears and her wishes: she thought the wise youth very wise: the poor child was not insensible to his flattery, and the subtler flattery of making herself in some measure a sacrifice to the home she had disturbed. She agreed to simulate as Adrian had suggested.

Victory is the commonest heritage of the hero, and when Richard came on shore proclaiming that the Blandish had beaten the Begum by seven minutes and three-quarters, he was hastily kissed and congratulated by his bride with her fingers among the leaves of Dr. Kitchener, and anxiously questioned about wine.

"Dearest! Mr. Harley wants to stay with us a little, and he thinks we ought not to go immediately—that is, before he has had some letters, and I feel… I would so much rather…"

"Ah! that's it, you coward!" said Richard. "Well, then, to-morrow. We had a splendid race. Did you see us?"

"Oh, yes! I saw you and was sure my darling would win." And again she threw on him the cold water of that solicitude about wine. "Mr. Harley must have the best, you know, and we never drink it, and I'm so silly, I don't know good wine, and if you would send Tom where he can get good wine. I have seen to the dinner."

"So that's why you didn't come to meet me?"

"Pardon me, darling."

Well, I do, but Mountfalcon doesn't, and Lady Judith thinks you ought to have been there."

"Ah, but my heart was with you!"

Richard put his hand to feel for the little heart: her eyelids softened, and she ran away.

It is to say much of the dinner that Adrian found no fault with it, and was in perfect good-humour at the conclusion of the service. He did not abuse the wine they were able to procure for him, which was also much. The coffee, too, had the honour of passing without comment. These were sound first steps toward the conquest of an epicure, and as yet Cupid did not grumble.

After coffee they strolled out to see the sun set from Lady Judith's grounds. The wind had dropped. The clouds had rolled from the zenith, and ranged in amphitheatre with distant flushed bodies over sea and land: Titanic crimson head and chest rising from the wave faced Hyperion falling. There hung Briareus with deep-indented trunk and ravined brows, stretching all his hands up to unattainable blue summits. North-west the range had a rich white glow, as if shining to the moon, and westward, streams of amber, melting into upper rose, shot out from the dipping disk.

"What Sandoe calls the passion-flower of heaven," said Richard under his breath to Adrian, who was serenely chanting Greek hexameters, and answered, in the swing of the caesura, "He might as well have said cauliflower."

Lady Judith, with a black lace veil tied over her head, met them in the walk. She was tall and dark; dark-haired, dark-eyed, sweet and persuasive in her accent and manner. "A second edition of the Blandish," thinks Adrian. She welcomed him as one who had claims on her affability. She kissed Lucy protectingly, and remarking on the wonders of the evening, appropriated her husband. Adrian and Lucy found themselves walking behind them.

The sun was under. All the spaces of the sky were alight, and Richard's fancy flamed.

> "So you're not intoxicated with your immense triumph
> this morning?" said Lady Judith

"Don't laugh at me. When it's over I feel ashamed of the trouble I've taken. Look at that glory!—I'm sure you despise me for it."

"Was I not there to applaud you? I only think such energies should be turned into some definitely useful channel. But you must not go into the Army."

"What else can I do?"

"You are fit for so much that is better."

"I never can be anything like Austin."

"But I think you can do more."

> "Well, I thank you for thinking it, Lady Judith.
> Something I will do.
> A man must deserve to live, as you say.

"Sauces," Adrian was heard to articulate distinctly in the rear, "Sauces are the top tree of this science. A woman who has mastered sauces sits on the apex of civilization."

Briareus reddened duskily seaward. The West was all a burning rose.

> "How can men see such sights as those, and live idle?"
> Richard resumed.
> "I feel ashamed of asking my men to work for me.—Or I
> feel so now."

"Not when you're racing the Begum, I think. There's no necessity for you to turn democrat like Austin. Do you write now?"

"No. What is writing like mine? It doesn't deceive me. I know it's only the excuse I'm making to myself for remaining idle. I haven't written a line since—lately."

"Because you are so happy."

"No, not because of that. Of course I'm very happy…" He did not finish.

Vague, shapeless ambition had replaced love in yonder skies. No Scientific Humanist was by to study the natural development, and guide him. This lady would hardly be deemed a very proper guide to the undirected energies of the youth, yet they had established relations of that nature. She was five years older than he, and a woman, which may explain her serene presumption.

The cloud-giants had broken up: a brawny shoulder smouldered over the sea.

"We'll work together in town, at all events," said Richard,

"Why can't we go about together at night and find out people who want help?"

Lady Judith smiled, and only corrected his nonsense by saying, "I think we mustn't be too romantic. You will become a knight-errant, I suppose. You have the characteristics of one."

"Especially at breakfast," Adrian's unnecessarily emphatic gastronomical lessons to the young wife here came in.

"You must be our champion," continued Lady Judith: "the rescuer and succourer of distressed dames and damsels. We want one badly."

"You do," said Richard, earnestly: "from what I hear: from what I know!" His thoughts flew off with him as knight-errant hailed shrilly at exceeding critical moment by distressed dames and damsels. Images of airy towers hung around. His fancy performed miraculous feats. The towers crumbled. The stars grew larger, seemed to throb with lustre. His fancy crumbled with the towers of the air, his heart gave a leap, he turned to Lucy.

"My darling! what have you been doing?" And as if to compensate her for his little knight-errant infidelity, he pressed very tenderly to her.

"We have been engaged in a charming conversation on domestic cookery," interposed Adrian.

> "Cookery! such an evening as this?" His face was a handsome likeness of Hippias at the presentation of bridecake.

"Dearest! you know it's very useful," Lucy mirthfully pleaded.

"Indeed I quite agree with you, child," said Lady Judith, and I think you have the laugh of us. I certainly will learn to cook some day."

"Woman's mission, in so many words," ejaculated Adrian.

"And pray, what is man's?"

"To taste thereof, and pronounce thereupon."

"Let us give it up to them," said Lady Judith to Richard. "You and I never will make so delightful and beautifully balanced a world of it."

Richard appeared to have grown perfectly willing to give everything up to the fair face, his bridal Hesper.

Neat day Lucy had to act the coward anew, and, as she did so, her heart sank to see how painfully it affected him that she should hesitate to go with him to his father. He was patient, gentle; he sat down by her side to appeal to her reason, and used all the arguments he could think of to persuade her.

"If we go together and make him see us both: if he sees he has nothing to be ashamed of in you—rather everything to be proud of; if you are only near him, you will not have to speak a word, and I'm certain—as certain as that I live—that in a week we shall be settled happily at Raynham. I know my father so well, Lucy. Nobody knows him but I."

Lucy asked whether Mr. Harley did not.

"Adrian? Not a bit. Adrian only knows a part of people, Lucy; and not the best part."

Lucy was disposed to think more highly of the object of her conquest.

"Is it he that has been frightening you, Lucy?"

"No, no, Richard; oh, dear no!" she cried, and looked at him more tenderly because she was not quite truthful.

"He doesn't know my father at all," said Richard. But Lucy had another opinion of the wise youth, and secretly maintained it. She could not be won to imagine the baronet a man of human mould, generous, forgiving, full of passionate love at heart, as Richard tried to picture him, and thought him, now that he beheld him again through Adrian's embassy. To her he was that awful figure, shrouded by the midnight. "Why are you so harsh?" she had heard Richard cry more than once. She was sure that Adrian must be right.

"Well, I tell you I won't go without you," said Richard, and Lucy begged for a little more time.

Cupid now began to grumble, and with cause. Adrian positively refused to go on the water unless that element were smooth as a plate. The South- west still joked boisterously at any comparison of the sort; the days were magnificent; Richard had yachting engagements; and Lucy always petitioned to stay to keep Adrian company, concerning it her duty as hostess. Arguing with Adrian was an absurd idea. If Richard hinted at his retaining Lucy, the wise youth would remark: "It's a wholesome interlude to your extremely Cupidinous behaviour, my dear boy."

Richard asked his wife what they could possibly find to talk about.

"All manner of things," said Lucy; "not only cookery. He is so amusing, though he does make fun of The Pilgrim's Scrip, and I think he ought not. And then, do you know, darling—you won't think me vain?—I think he is beginning to like me a little."

Richard laughed at the humble mind of his Beauty.

> "Doesn't everybody like you, admire you? Doesn't Lord Mountfalcon, and Mr. Morton, and Lady Judith?"

"But he is one of your family, Richard."

"And they all will, if she isn't a coward."

"Ah, no!" she sighs, and is chidden.

The conquest of an epicure, or any young wife's conquest beyond her husband, however loyally devised for their mutual happiness, may be costly to her. Richard in his hours of excitement was thrown very much with Lady Judith. He consulted her regarding what he termed Lucy's cowardice. Lady Judith said: "I think she's wrong, but you must learn to humour little women."

"Then would you advise me to go up alone?" he asked, with a cloudy forehead.

"What else can you do? Be reconciled yourself as
quickly as you can.
You can't drag her like a captive, you know?"

It is not pleasant for a young husband, fancying his bride the peerless flower of Creation, to learn that he must humour a little woman in her. It was revolting to Richard.

"What I fear," he said, "is, that my father will make it smooth with me, and not acknowledge her: so that whenever I go to him, I shall have to leave her, and tit for tat—an abominable existence, like a ball on a billiard-table. I won't bear that ignominy. And this I know, I know! she might prevent it at once, if she would only be brave, and face it. You, you, Lady Judith, you wouldn't be a coward?"

"Where my old lord tells me to go, I go," the lady coldly replied. "There's not much merit in that. Pray, don't cite me. Women are born cowards, you know."

"But I love the women who are not cowards."

"The little thing—your wife has not refused to go?"

"No—but tears! Who can stand tears?"

Lucy had come to drop them. Unaccustomed to have his will thwarted, and urgent where he saw the thing to do so clearly, the young husband had spoken strong words: and she, who knew that she would have given her life by inches for him; who knew that she was playing a part for his happiness, and hiding for his sake the nature that was worthy his esteem; the poor little martyr had been weak a moment.

She had Adrian's support. The wise youth was very comfortable. He liked the air of the Island, and he liked being petted. "A nice little woman! a very nice little woman!" Tom Bakewell heard him murmur to himself according to a habit he had; and his air of rather succulent patronage as he walked or sat beside the innocent Beauty, with his head thrown back and a smile that seemed always to be in secret communion with his marked abdominal prominence, showed that she was gaining part of what she played for. Wise youths who buy their loves, are not unwilling, when opportunity offers, to try and obtain the commodity for nothing. Examinations of her hand, as for some occult purpose, and unctuous pattings of the same, were not infrequent. Adrian waxed now and then Anacreontic in his compliments. Lucy would say: "That's worse than Lord Mountfalcon."

"Better English than the noble lord deigns to employ—
allow that?" quoth Adrian.

"He is very kind," said Lucy.

"To all, save to our noble vernacular," added Adrian. "He seems to scent a rival to his dignity there."

It may be that Adrian scented a rival to his lymphatic emotions.

"We are at our ease here in excellent society," he wrote to Lady Blandish. "I am bound to confess that the Huron has a happy fortune, or a superlative instinct. Blindfold he has seized upon a suitable mate. She can look at a lord, and cook for an epicure. Besides Dr. Kitchener, she reads and comments on The Pilgrim's Scrip. The `Love' chapter, of course, takes her fancy. That picture of Woman, `Drawn by Reverence and coloured by Love,' she thinks beautiful, and repeats it, tossing up pretty eyes. Also the lover's petition: 'Give me purity to be worthy the good in her, and grant her patience to reach the good in me.' 'Tis quite taking to hear her lisp it. Be sure that I am repeating the petition! I make her read me her choice passages. She has not a bad voice.

"The Lady Judith I spoke of is Austin's Miss Menteith, married to the incapable old Lord Felle, or Fellow, as the wits here call him. Lord Mountfalcon is his cousin, and her—what? She has been trying to find out, but they have both got over their perplexity, and act respectively the bad man reproved and the chaste counsellor; a position in which our young couple found them, and haply diverted its perils. They had quite taken them in hand. Lady Judith undertakes to cure the fair Papist of a pretty, modest trick of frowning and blushing when addressed, and his lordship directs the exuberant energies of the original man. 'Tis thus we fulfil our destinies, and are content. Sometimes they change pupils; my lord educates the little dame, and my lady the hope of Raynham. Joy and blessings unto all! as the German poet sings. Lady Judith accepted the hand of her decrepit lord that she might be of potent service to her fellow-creatures. Austin, you know, had great hopes of her.

"I have for the first time in my career a field of lords to study. I think it is not without meaning that I am introduced to it by a yeoman's niece. The language of the two social extremes is similar. I find it to consist in an instinctively lavish use of vowels and adjectives. My lord and Farmer Blaize speak the same tongue, only my lord's has lost its backbone, and is limp, though fluent. Their pursuits are identical; but that one has money, or, as the Pilgrim terms it, vantage, and the other has not. Their ideas seem to have a special relationship in the peculiarity of stopping where they have begun. Young Tom Blaize with vantage would be Lord Mountfalcon. Even in the character of their parasites I see a resemblance, though I am bound to confess that the Hon. Peter Brayder, who is my lord's parasite, is by no means noxious.

"This sounds dreadfully democrat. Pray, don't be alarmed. The discovery of the affinity between the two extremes of the Royal British Oak has made me thrice conservative. I see now that the national love of a lord is less subservience than a form of self-love; putting a gold-lace hat on one's image, as it were, to bow to it. I see, too, the admirable wisdom of our system:—could there be a finer balance of power than in a community where men intellectually nil, have lawful vantage and a gold- lace hat on? How soothing it is to intellect—that noble rebel, as the Pilgrim has it—to stand, and bow, and know itself superior! This exquisite compensation maintains the balance: whereas that period anticipated by the Pilgrim, when science shall have produced an intellectual aristocracy, is indeed horrible to contemplate. For what despotism is so black as one the mind cannot challenge? 'Twill be an iron Age. Wherefore, madam, I cry, and shall continue to cry, 'Vive Lord Mountfalcon! long may he sip his Burgundy! long may the bacon-fed carry him on their shoulders!'

"Mr. Morton (who does me the honour to call me Young Mephisto, and Socrates missed) leaves to-morrow to get Master Ralph out of a scrape. Our Richard has just been elected member of a Club for the promotion of nausea. Is he happy? you ask. As much so as one who has had the misfortune to obtain what he wanted can be. Speed is his passion. He races from point to point. In emulation of Leander and Don Juan, he swam, I hear, to the opposite shores the other day, or some world-shaking feat of the sort: himself the Hero whom he went to meet: or, as they who pun say, his Hero was a Bet. A pretty little domestic episode occurred this morning. He finds her abstracted in the fire of his caresses: she turns shy and seeks solitude: green jealousy takes hold of him: he lies in wait, and discovers her with his new rival—a veteran edition of the culinary Doctor! Blind to the Doctor's great national services, deaf to her wild music, he grasps the intruder, dismembers him, and performs upon him the treatment he has recommended for dressed cucumber. Tears and shrieks accompany the descent of the gastronome. Down she rushes to secure the cherished fragments: he follows: they find him, true to his character, alighted and straggling over a bed of blooming flowers. Yet ere a fairer flower can gather him, a heel black as Pluto stamps him into earth, flowers and all:—happy burial! Pathetic tribute to his merit is watering his grave, when by saunters my Lord Mountfalcon. 'What's the mattah?' says his lordship, soothing his moustache. They break apart, and 'tis left to me to explain from the window. My lord looks shocked, Richard is angry with her for having to be ashamed of himself, Beauty dries her eyes, and after a pause of general foolishness, the business of life is resumed. I may add that the Doctor has just been dug up, and we are busy, in the enemy's absence, renewing old Aeson with enchanted threads. By the way, a Papist priest has blest them."

A month had passed when Adrian wrote this letter. He was very comfortable; so of course he thought Time was doing his duty. Not a word did he say of Richard's return, and for some reason or other neither Richard nor Lucy spoke of it now.

> Lady Blandish wrote back: "His father thinks he has
> refused to come to him. By your utter silence on the
> subject, I fear that it must be so.
> Make him come. Bring him by force. Insist on his
> coming. Is he mad?
> He must come at once."
>
> To this Adrian replied, after a contemplative
> comfortable lapse of a day or two, which might be laid
> to his efforts to adopt the lady's advice,
> "The point is that the half man declines to come without
> the whole man.
> The terrible question of sex is our obstruction."

Lady Blandish was in despair. She had no positive assurance that the baronet would see his son; the mask put them all in the dark; but she thought she saw in Sir Austin irritation that the offender, at least when the opening to come and make his peace seemed to be before him, should let days and weeks go by. She saw through the mask sufficiently not to have any hope of his consenting to receive the couple at present; she was sure that his equanimity was fictitious; but she pierced no farther, or she might have started and asked herself, Is this the heart of a woman?

The lady at last wrote to Richard. She said: "Come instantly, and come alone." Then Richard, against his judgment, gave way. "My father is not the man I thought him!" he exclaimed sadly, and Lucy felt his eyes saying to her: "And you, too, are not the woman I thought you." Nothing could the poor little heart reply but strain to his bosom and sleeplessly pray in his arms all the night.

CHAPTER XXXV

Three weeks after Richard arrived in town, his cousin Clare was married, under the blessings of her energetic mother, and with the approbation of her kinsfolk, to the husband that had been expeditiously chosen for her. The gentleman, though something more than twice the age of his bride, had no idea of approaching senility for many long connubial years to come. Backed by his tailor and his hairdresser, he presented no such bad figure at the altar, and none would have thought that he was an ancient admirer of his bride's mama, as certainly none knew he had lately proposed for Mrs. Doria before there was any question of her daughter. These things were secrets; and the elastic and happy appearance of Mr. John Todhunter did not betray them at the altar. Perhaps he would rather have married the mother. He was a man of property, well born, tolerably well educated, and had, when Mrs. Doria rejected him for the first time, the reputation of being a fool—which a wealthy man may have in his youth; but as he lived on, and did not squander his money—amassed it, on the contrary, and did not seek to go into Parliament, and did other negative wise things, the world's opinion, as usual, veered completely round, and John Todhunter was esteemed a shrewd, sensible man—only not brilliant; that he was brilliant could not be said of him. In fact, the man could hardly talk, and it was a fortunate provision that no impromptu deliveries were required of him in the marriage-service.

Mrs. Doria had her own reasons for being in a hurry. She had discovered something of the strange impassive nature of her child; not from any confession of Clare's, but from signs a mother can read when, her eyes are not resolutely shut. She saw with alarm and anguish that Clare had fallen into the pit she had been digging for her so laboriously. In vain she entreated the baronet to break the disgraceful, and, as she said, illegal alliance his son had contracted. Sir Austin would not even stop the little pension to poor Berry. "At least you will do that, Austin," she begged pathetically. "You will show your sense of that horrid woman's conduct?" He refused to offer up any victim to console her. Then Mrs. Doria told him her thoughts,—and when an outraged energetic lady is finally brought to exhibit these painfully hoarded treasures, she does not use half words as a medium. His System, and his conduct generally were denounced to him, without analysis. She let him understand that the world laughed at him; and he heard this from her at a time when his mask was still soft and liable to be acted on by his nerves. "You are weak, Austin! weak, I tell you!" she said, and, like all angry and self-interested people, prophecy came easy to her. In her heart she accused him of her own fault, in imputing to him the wreck of her project. The baronet allowed her to revel in the proclamation of a dire future, and quietly counselled her to keep apart from him, which his sister assured him she would do.

But to be passive in calamity is the province of no woman. Mark the race at any hour. "What revolution and hubbub does not that little instrument, the needle, avert from us!" says The Pilgrim's Scrip. Alas, that in calamity women cannot stitch! Now that she saw Clare wanted other than iron, it struck her she must have a husband, and be made secure as a woman and a wife. This seemed the thing to do: and, as she had forced the iron down Clare's throat, so she forced the husband, and Clare gulped at the latter as she had at the former. On the very day that Mrs. Doria had this new track shaped out before her, John Todhunter called at the Foreys'. "Old John!" sang out Mrs. Doria, "show him up to me. I want to see him particularly." He sat with her alone. He was a man multitudes of women would have married—whom will they not?—and who would have married any presentable woman: but women do want asking, and John never had the word. The rape of such men is left to the practical animal. So John sat alone with his old flame. He had become resigned to her perpetual lamentation and living Suttee for his defunct rival. But, ha! what meant those soft glances now—addressed to him? His tailor and his hairdresser gave youth to John, but they had not the art to bestow upon him distinction, and an undistinguished man what woman looks at? John was an indistinguishable man. For that reason he was dry wood to a soft glance.

And now she said: "It is time you should marry; and you are the man to be the guide and helper of a young woman, John. You are well preserved—younger than most of the young men of our day. You are eminently domestic, a good son, and will be a good husband and good father. Some one you must marry.—What do you think of Clare for a wife for you?"

At first John Todhunter thought it would be very much like his marrying a baby. However, he listened to it, and that was enough for Mrs. Doria.

She went down to John's mother, and consulted with her on the propriety of the scheme of wedding her daughter to John in accordance with his proposition. Mrs. Todhunter's jealousy of any disturbing force in the influence she held over her son Mrs. Doria knew to be one of the causes of John's remaining constant to the impression she had afore-time produced on him. She spoke so kindly of John, and laid so much stress on the ingrained obedience and passive disposition of her daughter, that Mrs. Todhunter was led to admit she did think it almost time John should be seeking a mate, and that he—all things considered—would hardly find a fitter one. And this, John Todhunter—old John no more—heard to his amazement when, a day or two subsequently, he instanced the probable disapproval of his mother.

The match was arranged. Mrs. Doria did the wooing. It consisted in telling Clare that she had come to years when marriage was desirable, and that she had fallen into habits of moping which might have the worse effect on her future life, as it had on her present health and appearance, and which a husband would cure. Richard was told by Mrs. Doria that Clare had instantaneously consented to accept Mr. John Todhunter as lord of her days, and with more than obedience—with alacrity. At all events, when Richard spoke to Clare, the strange passive creature did not admit constraint on her inclinations. Mrs. Doria allowed Richard to speak to her. She laughed at his futile endeavours to undo her work, and the boyish sentiments he uttered on the subject. "Let us see, child," she said, "let us see which turns out the best; a marriage of passion, or a marriage of common sense."

Heroic efforts were not wanting to arrest the union. Richard made repeated journeys to Hounslow, where Ralph was quartered, and if Ralph could have been persuaded to carry off a young lady who did not love him, from the bridegroom her mother averred she did love, Mrs. Doria might have been defeated. But Ralph in his cavalry quarters was cooler than Ralph in the Bursley meadows. "Women are oddities, Dick," he remarked, running a finger right and left along his upper lip. "Best leave them to their own freaks. She's a dear girl, though she doesn't talk: I like her for that. If she cared for me I'd go the race. She never did. It's no use asking a girl twice. She knows whether she cares a fig for a fellow."

The hero quitted him with some contempt, As Ralph Morton was a young man, and he had determined that John Todhunter was an old man, he sought another private interview with Clare, and getting her alone, said: "Clare, I've come to you for the last time. Will you marry Ralph Morton?"

To which Clare replied, "I cannot marry two husbands, Richard."

"Will you refuse to marry this old man?"

"I must do as mama wishes."

"Then you're going to marry an old man—a man you don't love, and can't love! Oh, good God! do you know what you're doing?" He flung about in a fury. "Do you know what it is? Clare!" he caught her two hands violently, "have you any idea of the horror you're going to commit?"

She shrank a little at his vehemence, but neither blushed nor stammered: answering: "I see nothing wrong in doing what mama thinks right, Richard."

"Your mother! I tell you it's an infamy, Clare! It's a miserable sin! I tell you, if I had done such a thing I would not live an hour after it. And coldly to prepare for it! to be busy about your dresses! They told me when I came in that you were with the milliner. To be smiling over the horrible outrage! decorating yourself!"...

"Dear Richard," said Clare, "you will make me very unhappy."

"That one of my blood should be so debased!" he cried, brushing angrily at his face. "Unhappy! I beg you to feel for yourself, Clare. But I suppose," and he said it scornfully, "girls don't feel this sort of shame."

She grew a trifle paler.

"Next to mama, I would wish to please you, dear Richard."

"Have you no will of your own?" he exclaimed.

She looked at him softly; a look he interpreted for the meekness he detested in her.

"No, I believe you have none!" he added. "And what can I do? I can't step forward and stop this accursed marriage. If you would but say a word I would save you; but you tie my hands. And they expect me to stand by and see it done!"

"Will you not be there, Richard?" said Clare, following the question with her soft eyes. It was the same voice that had so thrilled him on his marriage morn.

"Oh, my darling Clare!" he cried in the kindest way he had ever used to her, "if you knew how I feel this!" and now as he wept she wept, and came insensibly into his arms.

"My darling Clare!" he repeated.

She said nothing, but seemed to shudder, weeping.

"You will do it, Clare? You will be sacrificed? So lovely as you are, too!... Clare! you cannot be quite blind. If I dared speak to you, and tell you all.... Look up. Can you still consent?"

"I must not disobey mama," Clare murmured, without looking up from the nest her cheek had made on his bosom.

"Then kiss me for the last time," said Richard. "I'll never kiss you after it, Clare."

He bent his head to meet her mouth, and she threw her arms wildly round him, and kissed him convulsively, and clung to his lips, shutting her eyes, her face suffused with a burning red.

Then he left her, unaware of the meaning of those passionate kisses.

Argument with Mrs. Doria was like firing paper-pellets against a stone wall. To her indeed the young married hero spoke almost indecorously, and that which his delicacy withheld him from speaking to Clare. He could provoke nothing more responsive from the practical animal than "Pooh-pooh! Tush, tush! and Fiddlededee!"

"Really," Mrs. Doria said to her intimates, "that boy's education acts like a disease on him. He cannot regard anything sensibly. He is for ever in some mad excess of his fancy, and what he will come to at last heaven only knows! I sincerely pray that Austin will be able to bear it."

Threats of prayer, however, that harp upon their sincerity, are not very well worth having. Mrs. Doria had embarked in a practical controversy, as it were, with her brother. Doubtless she did trust he would be able to bear his sorrows to come, but one who has uttered prophecy can barely help hoping to see it fulfilled: she had prophecied much grief to the baronet.

Poor John Todhunter, who would rather have married the mother, and had none of your heroic notions about the sacred necessity for love in marriage, moved as one guiltless of offence, and deserving his happiness. Mrs. Doria shielded him from the hero. To see him smile at Clare's obedient figure, and try not to look paternal, was touching.

Meantime Clare's marriage served one purpose. It completely occupied Richard's mind, and prevented him from chafing at the vexation of not finding his father ready to meet him when he came to town. A letter had awaited Adrian at the hotel, which said, "Detain him till you hear further from me. Take him about with you into every form of society." No more than that. Adrian had to extemporize, that the baronet had gone down to Wales on pressing business, and would be back in a week or so. For ulterior inventions and devices wherewith to keep the young gentleman in town, he applied to Mrs. Doria. "Leave him to me," said Mrs. Doria, "I'll manage him." And she did.

"Who can say," asks The Pilgrim's Scrip, "when he is not walking a puppet to some woman?"

Mrs. Doria would hear no good of Lucy. "I believe," she observed, as Adrian ventured a shrugging protest in her behalf,—"it is my firm opinion, that a scullery-maid would turn any of you men round her little finger—only give her time and opportunity." By dwelling on the arts of women, she reconciled it to her conscience to do her best to divide the young husband from his wife till it pleased his father they should live their unhallowed union again. Without compunction, or a sense of incongruity, she abused her brother and assisted the fulfilment of his behests.

So the puppets were marshalled by Mrs. Doria, happy, or sad, or indifferent. Quite against his set resolve and the tide of his feelings, Richard found himself standing behind Clare in the church—the very edifice that had witnessed his own marriage, and heard, "I, Clare Doria, take thee John

Pemberton," clearly pronounced. He stood with black brows dissecting the arts of the tailor and hairdresser on unconscious John. The back, and much of the middle, of Mr. Todhunter's head was bald; the back shone like an egg-shell, but across the middle the artist had drawn two long dabs of hair from the sides, and plastered them cunningly, so that all save wilful eyes would have acknowledged the head to be covered. The man's only pretension was to a respectable juvenility. He had a good chest, stout limbs, a face inclined to be jolly. Mrs. Doria had no cause to be put out of countenance at all by the exterior of her son-in-law: nor was she. Her splendid hair and gratified smile made a light in the church. Playing puppets must be an immense pleasure to the practical animal. The Forey bridesmaids, five in number, and one Miss Doria, their cousin, stood as girls do stand at these sacrifices, whether happy, sad, or indifferent; a smile on their lips and tears in attendance. Old Mrs. Todhunter, an exceedingly small ancient woman, was also there. "I can't have my boy John married without seeing it done," she said, and throughout the ceremony she was muttering audible encomiums on her John's manly behaviour.

The ring was affixed to Clare's finger; there was no ring lost in this common-sense marriage. The instant the clergyman bade him employ it, John drew the ring out, and dropped it on the finger of the cold passive hand in a businesslike way, as one who had studied the matter. Mrs. Doria glanced aside at Richard. Richard observed Clare spread out her fingers that the operation might be the more easily effected.

He did duty in the vestry a few minutes, and then said to his aunt:

"Now I'll go."

"You'll come to the breakfast, child? The Foreys"—

He cut her short. "I've stood for the family, and I'll do no more. I won't pretend to eat and make merry over it."

"Richard!"

"Good-bye."

She had attained her object and she wisely gave way.

"Well. Go and kiss Clare, and shake his hand. Pray, pray be civil."

She turned to Adrian, and said: "He is going. You must go with him, and find some means of keeping him, or he'll be running off to that woman. Now, no words—go!"

Richard bade Clare farewell. She put up her mouth to him humbly, but he kissed her on the forehead.

"Do not cease to love me," she said in a quavering whisper in his ear.

Mr. Todhunter stood beaming and endangering the art of the hairdresser with his pocket-handkerchief. Now he positively was married, he thought he would rather have the daughter than the mother, which is a reverse of the order of human thankfulness at a gift of the Gods.

"Richard, my boy!" he said heartily, "congratulate me."

"I should be happy to, if I could," sedately replied the hero, to the consternation of those around. Nodding to the bridesmaids and bowing to the old lady, he passed out.

Adrian, who had been behind him, deputed to watch for a possible unpleasantness, just hinted to John: "You know, poor fellow, he has got into a mess with his marriage."

"Oh! ah! yes!" kindly said John, "poor fellow!"

All the puppets then rolled off to the breakfast.

Adrian hurried after Richard in an extremely discontented state of mind. Not to be at the breakfast and see the best of the fun, disgusted him. However, he remembered that he was a philosopher, and the strong disgust he felt was only expressed in concentrated cynicism on every earthly matter engendered by the conversation. They walked side by side into Kensington Gardens. The hero was mouthing away to himself, talking by fits.

Presently he faced Adrian, crying: "And I might have stopped it! I see it now! I might have stopped it by going straight to him, and asking him if he dared marry a girl who did not love him. And I never thought of it. Good heaven! I feel this miserable affair on my conscience."

"Ah!" groaned Adrian. "An unpleasant cargo for the conscience, that! I would rather carry anything on mine than a married couple. Do you purpose going to him now?"

The hero soliloquized: "He's not a bad sort of man."...

"Well, he's not a Cavalier," said Adrian, "and that's why you wonder your aunt selected him, no doubt? He's decidedly of the Roundhead type, with the Puritan extracted, or inoffensive, if latent."

"There's the double infamy!" cried Richard, "that a man you can't call bad, should do this damned thing!"

"Well, it's hard we can't find a villain."

"He would have listened to me, I'm sure."

"Go to him now, Richard, my son. Go to him now. It's not yet too late. Who knows? If he really has a noble elevated superior mind—though not a Cavalier in person, he may be one at heart—he might, to please you, and since you put such stress upon it, abstain...perhaps with some loss of dignity, but never mind. And the request might be singular, or seem so, but everything has happened before in this world, you know, my dear boy. And what an infinite consolation it is for the eccentric, that reflection!"

The hero was impervious to the wise youth. He stared at him as if he were but a speck in the universe he visioned.

It was provoking that Richard should be Adrian's best subject for cynical pastime, in the extraordinary heterodoxies he started, and his worst in the way he took it; and the wise youth, against his will, had to feel as conscious of the young man's imaginative mental armour, as he was of his muscular physical.

"The same sort of day!" mused Richard, looking up. "I suppose my father's right. We make our own fates, and nature has nothing to do with it."

Adrian yawned.

"Some difference in the trees, though," Richard continued abstractedly.

"Growing bald at the top," said Adrian.

"Will you believe that my aunt Helen compared the conduct of that wretched slave Clare to Lucy's, who, she had the cruel insolence to say, entangled me into marriage?" the hero broke out loudly and rapidly. "You know—I told you, Adrian—how I had to threaten and insist, and how she pleaded, and implored me to wait."

"Ah! hum!" mumbled Adrian.

"You remember my telling you?" Richard was earnest to hear her exonerated.

"Pleaded and implored, my dear boy? Oh, no doubt she did. Where's the lass that doesn't."

"Call my wife by another name, if you please."

"The generic title can't be cancelled because of your having married one of the body, my son."

"She did all she could to persuade me to wait!" emphasized Richard.

Adrian shook his head with a deplorable smile.

"Come, come, my good Ricky; not all! not all!"

Richard bellowed: "What more could she have done?"

"She could have shaved her head, for instance."

This happy shaft did stick. With a furious exclamation Richard shot in front, Adrian following him; and asking him (merely to have his assumption verified), whether he did not think she might have shaved her head? and, presuming her to have done so, whether, in candour, he did not think he would have waited—at least till she looked less of a rank lunatic?

After a minute or so, the wise youth was but a fly buzzing about Richard's head. Three weeks of separation from Lucy, and an excitement deceased, caused him to have soft yearnings for the dear lovely home-face. He told Adrian it was his intention to go down that night. Adrian immediately became serious. He was at a loss what to invent to detain him, beyond the stale fiction that his father was coming to-morrow. He rendered homage to the genius of woman in these straits. "My aunt," he thought, "would have the lie ready; and not only that, but she would take care it did its work."

At this juncture the voice of a cavalier in the Row hailed them, proving to be the Honourable Peter Brayder, Lord Mountfalcon's parasite. He greeted them very cordially; and Richard, remembering some fun they had in the Island, asked him to dine with them; postponing his return till the next day. Lucy was his. It was even sweet to dally with the delight of seeing her.

The Hon. Peter was one who did honour to the body he belonged to. Though not so tall as a west of London footman, he was as shapely; and he had a power of making his voice insinuating, or arrogant, as it suited the exigencies of his profession. He had not a rap of money in the world; yet he rode a horse, lived high, expended largely. The world said that the Hon. Peter was salaried by his Lordship, and that, in common with that of Parasite, he exercised the ancient companion profession. This the world said, and still smiled at the Hon. Peter; for he was an engaging fellow, and where he went not Lord Mountfalcon would not go.

They had a quiet little hotel dinner, ordered by Adrian, and made a square at the table, Ripton Thompson being the fourth. Richard sent down to his office to fetch him, and the two friends shook hands for the first time since the great deed had been executed. Deep was the Old Dog's delight to hear the praises of his Beauty sounded by such aristocratic lips as the Hon. Peter Brayder's. All through the dinner he was throwing out hints and small queries to get a fuller account of her; and when the claret had circulated, he spoke a word or two himself, and heard the Hon. Peter eulogize his taste, and wish him a bride as beautiful; at which Ripton blushed, and said, he had no hope of that, and the Hon. Peter assured him marriage did not break the mould.

After the wine this gentleman took his cigar on the balcony, and found occasion to get some conversation with Adrian alone.

"Our young friend here—made it all right with the governor?" he asked carelessly.

"Oh yes!" said Adrian. But it struck him that Brayder might be of assistance in showing Richard a little of the `society in every form' required by his chief's prescript. "That is," he continued, "we are not yet permitted an interview with the august author of our being, and I have rather a difficult post. 'Tis mine both to keep him here, and also to find him the opportunity to measure himself with his fellow-man. In other words, his father wants him to see something of life before he enters upon housekeeping. Now I am proud to confess that I'm hardly equal to the task. The demi, or damnedmonde—if it's that lie wants him to observe—is one that I leave not got the walk to."

"Ha! ha!" laughed Brayder. "You do the keeping, I offer to parade the demi. I must say, though, it's a queer notion of the old gentleman."

"It's the continuation of a philosophic plan," said Adrian.

Brayder followed the curvings of the whiff of his cigar with his eyes, and ejaculated, "Infernally philosophic!"

"Has Lord Mountfalcon left the island?" Adrian inquired.

"Mount? to tell the truth I don't know where he is. Chasing some light craft, I suppose. That's poor Mount's weakness. It's his ruin, poor fellow! He's so confoundedly in earnest at the game."

"He ought to know it by this time, if fame speaks true," remarked Adrian.

"He's a baby about women, and always will be," said Brayder. "He's been once or twice wanting to marry them. Now there's a woman—you've heard of Mrs. Mount? All the world knows her.—If that woman hadn't scandalized."—The young man joined them, and checked the communication. Brayder winked to Adrian, and pitifully indicated the presence of an innocent.

"A married man, you know," said Adrian.

"Yes, yes!—we won't shock him," Brayder observed. He appeared to study the young man while they talked.

Next morning Richard was surprised by a visit from his aunt. Mrs. Doria took a seat by his side and spoke as follows:

"My dear nephew. Now you know I have always loved you, and thought of your welfare as if you had been my own child. More than that, I fear. Well, now, you are thinking of returning to—to that place—are you not? Yes. It is as I thought. Very well now, let me speak to you. You are in a much more dangerous position than you imagine. I don't deny your father's affection for you. It would be absurd to deny it. But you are of an age now to appreciate his character. Whatever you may do he will always give you money. That you are sure of; that you know. Very well. But you are one to want more than money: you want his love. Richard, I am convinced you will never be happy, whatever base pleasures you may be led into, if he should withhold his love from you. Now, child, you know you have grievously offended him. I wish not to animadvert on your conduct.—You fancied yourself in love, and so on, and you were rash. The less said of it the better now. But you must now—it is your duty now to do something—to do everything that lies in your power to show him you repent. No interruptions! Listen to me. You must consider him. Austin is not like other men. Austin requires the most delicate management. You must—whether you feel it or no—present an appearance of contrition. I counsel it for the good of all. He is just like a woman, and where his feelings are offended he wants utter subservience. He has you in town, and he does not see you:—now you know that he and I are not in communication: we have likewise our differences:—Well, he has you in town, and he holds aloof:—he is trying you, my dear Richard. No: he is not at Raynham: I do not know where he is. He is trying you, child, and you must be patient. You must convince him that you do not care utterly for your own gratification. If this person—I wish to speak of her with respect, for your sake—well, if she loves you at all—if, I say, she loves you one atom, she will repeat my solicitations for you to stay and patiently wait here till he consents to see you. I tell you candidly, it's your only chance of ever getting him to receive her. That you should know. And now, Richard, I may add that there is something else you should know. You should know that it depends entirely upon your conduct now, whether you are to see your father's heart for ever divided from you, and a new family at Raynham. You do not understand? I will explain. Brothers and sisters are excellent things for young people, but a new brood of them can hardly be acceptable to a young man. In fact, they are, and must be, aliens. I only tell you what I have heard on good authority. Don't you understand now? Foolish boy! if you do not humour him, he will marry her. Oh! I am sure of it. I know it. And this you will drive him to. I do not warn you on the score of your prospects, but of your feelings. I should regard such a contingency, Richard, as a final division between you. Think of the scandal! but alas, that is the least of the evils."

It was Mrs. Doria's object to produce an impression, and avoid an argument. She therefore left him as soon as she had, as she supposed, made her mark on the young man. Richard was very silent during the speech, and save for an exclamation or so, had listened attentively. He pondered on what his aunt said. He loved Lady Blandish, and yet he did not wish to see her Lady Feverel. Mrs. Doria laid painful stress on the scandal, and though he did not give his mind to this, he thought of it. He thought of his mother. Where was she? But most his thoughts recurred to his father, and something akin to jealousy slowly awakened his heart to him. He had given him up, and had not latterly felt extremely filial; but he could not bear the idea of a division in the love of which he had ever been the idol and sole object. And such a man, too! so good! so generous! If it was jealousy that roused the young man's heart to his father, the better part of love was also revived in it. He thought of old days: of his father's forbearance, his own wilfulness. He looked on himself, and what he had done, with the eyes of such a man. He determined to do all he could to regain his favour.

Mrs. Doria learnt from Adrian in the evening that her nephew intended waiting in town another week.

"That will do," smiled Mrs. Doria. "He will be more patient at the end of a week."

"Oh! does patience beget patience?" said Adrian. "I was not aware it was a propagating virtue. I surrender him to you. I shan't be able to hold him in after one week more. I assure you, my dear aunt, he's already"...

"Thank you, no explanation," Mrs. Doria begged.

When Richard saw her nest, he was informed that she had received a most satisfactory letter from Mrs. John Todhunter: quite a glowing account of John's behaviour: but on Richard's desiring to know the words Clare had written, Mrs. Doria objected to be explicit, and shot into worldly gossip.

"Clare seldom glows," said Richard.

"No, I mean for her," his aunt remarked. "Don't look like your father, child."

"I should like to have seen the letter," said Richard.

Mrs. Doria did not propose to show it.

CHAPTER XXXVI

A Lady driving a pair of greys was noticed by Richard in his rides and walks. She passed him rather obviously and often. She was very handsome; a bold beauty, with shining black hair, red lips, and eyes not afraid of men. The hair was brushed from her temples, leaving one of those fine reckless outlines which the action of driving, and the pace, admirably set off. She took his fancy. He liked the air of petulant gallantry about her, and mused upon the picture, rare to him, of a glorious dashing woman. He thought, too, she looked at him. He was not at the time inclined to be vain, or he might have been sure she did. Once it struck him she nodded slightly.

He asked Adrian one day in the park—who she was.

> "I don't know her," said Adrian. "Probably a superior priestess of Paphos."

"Now that's my idea of Bellona," Richard exclaimed. "Not the fury they paint, but a spirited, dauntless, eager-looking creature like that."

"Bellona?" returned the wise youth. "I don't think her hair was black. Red, wasn't it? I shouldn't compare her to Bellona; though, no doubt, she's as ready to spill blood. Look at her! She does seem to scent carnage. I see your idea. No; I should liken her to Diana emerged from the tutorship of Master Endymion, and at nice play among the gods. Depend upon it—they tell us nothing of the matter—Olympus shrouds the story—but you may be certain that when she left the pretty shepherd she had greater vogue than Venus up aloft."

Brayder joined them.

"See Mrs. Mount go by?" he said.

"Oh, that's Mrs. Mount!" cried Adrian.

"Who's Mrs. Mount?" Richard inquired.

"A sister to Miss Random, my dear boy."

"Like to know her?" drawled the Hon. Peter.

Richard replied indifferently, "No," and Mrs. Mount passed out of sight and out of the conversation.

The young man wrote submissive letters to his father. "I have remained here waiting to see you now five weeks," he wrote. "I have written to you three letters, and you do not reply to them. Let me tell you again how sincerely I desire and pray that you will come, or permit me to come to you and throw myself at your feet, and beg my forgiveness, and hers. She as earnestly implores it. Indeed, I am very wretched, sir. Believe me, there is nothing I would not do to regain your esteem and the love I fear I have unhappily forfeited. I will remain another week in the hope of hearing from you, or seeing you. I beg of you, sir, not to drive me mad. Whatever you ask of me I will consent to."

"Nothing he would not do!" the baronet commented as he read. "There is nothing he would not do! He will remain another week and give me that final chance! And it is I who drive him mad! Already he is beginning to cast his retribution on my shoulders."

Sir Austin had really gone down to Wales to be out of the way. A Shaddock-Dogmatist does not meet misfortune without hearing of it, and the author of The Pilgrim'S Scrip in trouble found London too hot for him. He quitted London to take refuge among the mountains; living there in solitary commune with a virgin Note-book.

Some indefinite scheme was in his head in this treatment of his son. Had he construed it, it would have looked ugly; and it settled to a vague principle that the young man should be tried and tested.

"Let him learn to deny himself something. Let him live with his equals for a term. If he loves me he will read my wishes." Thus he explained his principle to Lady Blandish.

The lady wrote: "You speak of a term. Till when? May I name one to him? It is the dreadful uncertainty that reduces him to despair. That, and nothing else. Pray be explicit."

In return, he distantly indicated Richard's majority.

How could Lady Blandish go and ask the young man to wait a year away from his wife? Her instinct began to open a wide eye on the idol she worshipped.

When people do not themselves know what they mean, they succeed in deceiving and imposing upon others. Not only was Lady Blandish mystified; Mrs. Doria, who pierced into the recesses of everybody's mind, and had always been in the habit of reading off her brother from infancy, and had never known herself to be once wrong about him, she confessed she was quite at a loss to comprehend Austin's principle. "For principle he has," said Mrs. Doria; "he never acts without one. But what it is, I cannot at present perceive. If he would write, and command the boy to await his return, all would be clear. He allows us to go and fetch him, and then leaves us all in a quandary. It must be some woman's influence. That is the only way to account for it."

"Singular!" interjected Adrian, "what pride women have in their sex! Well, I have to tell you, my dear aunt, that the day after to-morrow I hand my charge over to your keeping. I can't hold him in an hour longer. I've had to leash him with lies till my invention's exhausted. I petition to have them put down to the chief's account, but when the stream runs dry I can do no more. The last was, that I had heard from him desiring me to have the South-west bedroom ready for him on Tuesday proximate. 'So!' says my son, 'I'll wait till then,' and from the gigantic effort he exhibited in coming to it, I doubt any human power's getting him to wait longer."

"We must, we must detain him," said Mrs. Doria. "If we do not, I am convinced Austin will do something rash that he will for ever repent. He will marry that woman, Adrian. Mark my words. Now with any other young man!... But Richard's education! that ridiculous System!... Has he no distraction? nothing to amuse him?"

"Poor boy! I suppose he wants his own particular playfellow."

The wise youth had to bow to a reproof.

"I tell you, Adrian, he will marry that woman."

"My dear aunt! Can a chaste man do aught more commendable?"

"Has the boy no object we can induce him to follow?—If he had but a profession!"

"What say you to the regeneration of the streets of London, and the profession of moral-scavenger, aunt? I assure you I have served a month's apprenticeship with him. We sally forth on the tenth hour of the night. A female passes. I hear him groan. 'Is she one of them, Adrian?' I am compelled to admit she is not the saint he deems it the portion of every creature wearing petticoats to be. Another groan; an evident internal, 'It cannot be—and yet!'...that we hear on the stage. Rollings of eyes: impious questionings of the Creator of the universe; savage mutterings against brutal males; and then we meet a second young person, and repeat the performance—of which I am rather tired. It would be all very well, but he turns upon me, and lectures me because I don't hire a house, and furnish it for all the women one meets to live in in purity. Now that's too much to ask of a quiet man. Master Thompson has latterly relieved me, I'm happy to say."

Mrs. Doria thought her thoughts.

"Has Austin written to you since you were in town?"

"Not an Aphorism!" returned Adrian.

"I must see Richard to-morrow morning," Mrs. Doria ended the colloquy by saying.

The result of her interview with her nephew was, that Richard made no allusion to a departure on the Tuesday; and for many days afterward he appeared to have an absorbing business on his hands: but what it was Adrian did not then learn, and his admiration of Mrs. Doria's genius for management rose to a very high pitch.

> On a morning in October they had an early visitor in the person of the Hon. Peter, whom they had not seen for a week or more.
>
> "Gentlemen," he said, flourishing his cane in his most affable manner,
> "I've come to propose to you to join us in a little dinner-party at Richmond. Nobody's in town, you know.
> London's as dead as a stock-fish.
> Nothing but the scrapings to offer you. But the weather's fine: I flatter myself you'll find the company agreeable, What says my friend Feverel?"

Richard begged to be excused.

"No, no: positively you must come," said the Hon. Peter. "I've had some trouble to get them together to relieve the dulness of your incarceration. Richmond's within the rules of your prison. You can be back by night. Moonlight on the water—lovely woman. We've engaged a city-barge to pull us back. Eight oars—I'm not sure it isn't sixteen. Come—the word!"

Adrian was for going. Richard said he had an appointment with Ripton.

"You're in for another rick, you two," said Adrian. "Arrange that we go. You haven't seen the cockney's Paradise. Abjure Blazes, and taste of peace, my son."

After some persuasion, Richard yawned wearily, and got up, and threw aside the care that was on him, saying, "Very well. Just as you like. We'll take old Rip with us."

Adrian consulted Brayder's eye at this. The Hon. Peter briskly declared he should be delighted to have Feverel's friend, and offered to take them all down in his drag.

"If you don't get a match on to swim there with the tide—eh, Feverel, my boy?"

Richard replied that he had given up that sort of thing, at which Brayder communicated a queer glance to Adrian, and applauded the youth.

Richmond was under a still October sun. The pleasant landscape, bathed in Autumn, stretched from the foot of the hill to a red horizon haze. The day was like none that Richard vividly remembered. It touched no link in the chain of his recollection. It was quiet, and belonged to the spirit of the season.

Adrian had divined the character of the scrapings they were to meet. Brayder introduced them to one or two of the men, hastily and in rather an undervoice, as a thing to get over. They made their bow to the first knot of ladies they encountered. Propriety was observed strictly, even to severity. The general talk was of the weather. Here and there a lady would seize a button-hole or any little bit of the habiliments, of the man she was addressing; and if it came to her to chide him, she did it with more than a forefinger. This, however, was only here and there, and a privilege of intimacy.

Where ladies are gathered together, the Queen of the assemblage may be known by her Court of males. The Queen of the present gathering leaned against a corner of the open window, surrounded by a stalwart Court, in whom a practised eye would have discerned guardsmen, and Ripton, with a sinking of the heart, apprehended lords. They were fine men, offering inanimate homage. The trim of their whiskerage, the cut of their coats, the high-bred indolence in their aspect, eclipsed Ripton's sense of self-esteem. But they kindly looked over him. Occasionally one committed a momentary outrage on him with an eye-glass, seeming to cry out in a voice of scathing scorn, "Who's this?" and Ripton got closer to his hero to justify his humble pretensions to existence and an identity in the shadow of him. Richard gazed about. Heroes do not always know what to say or do; and the cold bath before dinner in strange company is one of the instances. He had recognized his superb Bellona in the lady by the garden window. For Brayder the men had nods and yokes, the ladies a pretty playfulness. He was very busy, passing between the groups, chatting, laughing, taking the feminine taps he received, and sometimes returning them in sly whispers. Adrian sat down and crossed his legs, looking amused and benignant.

"Whose dinner is it?" Ripton heard a mignonne beauty ask of a cavalier.

"Mount's, I suppose," was the answer.

"Where is he? Why don't he come?"

"An affaire, I fancy."

"There he is again! How shamefully he treats Mrs. Mount!"

"She don't seem to cry over it."

Mrs. Mount was flashing her teeth and eyes with laughter at one of her Court, who appeared to be Fool.

Dinner was announced. The ladies proclaimed extravagant appetites. Brayder posted his three friends. Ripton found himself under the lee of a dame with a bosom. On the other aide of him was the mignonne. Adrian was at the lower end of the table. Ladies were in profusion, and he had his share. Brayder drew Richard from seat to seat. A happy man had established himself next to Mrs. Mount. Him Brayder hailed to take the head of the table. The happy man objected, Brayder continued urgent, the lady tenderly insisted, the happy man grimaced, dropped into the post of honour, strove to look placable. Richard usurped his chair, and was not badly welcomed by his neighbour.

Then the dinner commenced, and had all the attention of the company, till the flying of the first champagne-cork gave the signal, and a hum began to spread. Sparkling wine, that looseneth the tongue, and displayeth the verity, hath also the quality of colouring it. The ladies laughed high; Richard only thought them gay and natural. They flung back in their chairs and laughed to tears; Ripton thought only of the pleasure he had in their society. The champagne-corks continued a regular file-firing.

> "Where have you been lately? I haven't seen you in the park," said Mrs. Mount to Richard.

"No," he replied, "I've not been there." The question seemed odd: she spoke so simply that it did not impress him. He emptied his glass, and had it filled again.

The Hon. Peter did most of the open talking, which related to horses, yachting, opera, and sport generally: who was ruined; by what horse, or by what woman. He told one or two of Richard's feats. Fair smiles rewarded the hero.

"Do you bet?" said Mrs. Mount.

"Only on myself," returned Richard.

"Bravo!" cried his Bellona, and her eye sent a lingering delirious sparkle across her brimming glass at him.

"I'm sure you're a safe one to back," she added, and seemed to scan his points approvingly.

Richard's cheeks mounted bloom.

"Don't you adore champagne?" quoth the dame with a bosom to Ripton.

"Oh, yes!" answered Ripton, with more candour than accuracy, "I always drink it."

"Do you indeed?" said the enraptured bosom, ogling him. "You would be a friend, now! I hope you don't object to a lady joining you now and then. Champagne's my folly."

A laugh was circling among the ladies of whom Adrian was the centre; first low, and as he continued some narration, peals resounded, till those excluded from the fun demanded the cue, and ladies leaned behind gentlemen to take it up, and formed an electric chain of laughter. Each one, as her ear received it, caught up her handkerchief, and laughed, and looked shocked afterwards, or looked shocked and then spouted laughter. The anecdote might have been communicated to the bewildered cavaliers, but coming to a lady of a demurer cast, she looked shocked without laughing, and reproved the female table, in whose breasts it was consigned to burial: but here and there a man's head was seen bent, and a lady's mouth moved, though her face was not turned toward him, and a man's broad laugh was presently heard, while the lady gazed unconsciously before her, and preserved her gravity if she could escape any other lady's eyes; failing in which, handkerchiefs were simultaneously seized, and a second chime arose, till the tickling force subsided to a few chance bursts.

What nonsense it is that my father writes about women! thought Richard. He says they can't laugh, and don't understand humour. It comes, he reflected, of his shutting himself from the world. And the idea that he was seeing the world, and feeling wiser, flattered him. He talked fluently to his dangerous Bellona. He gave her some reminiscences of Adrian's whimsies.

"Oh!" said she, "that's your tutor, is it!" She eyed the young man as if she thought he must go far and fast.

Ripton felt a push. "Look at that," said the bosom, fuming utter disgust. He was directed to see a manly arm round the waist of the mignonne. "Now that's what I don't like in company," the bosom inflated to observe with sufficient emphasis. "She always will allow it with everybody. Give her a nudge."

Ripton protested that he dared not; upon which she said, "Then I will"; and inclined her sumptuous bust across his lap, breathing wine in his face, and gave the nudge. The mignonne turned an inquiring eye on Ripton; a mischievous spark shot from it. She laughed, and said; "Aren't you satisfied with the old girl?"

"Impudence!" muttered the bosom, growing grander and redder.

"Do, do fill her glass, and keep her quiet—she drinks port when there's no more champagne," said the mignonne.

The bosom revenged herself by whispering to Ripton scandal of the mignonne, and between them he was enabled to form a correcter estimate of the company, and quite recovered from his original awe: so much so as to feel a touch of jealousy at seeing his lively little neighbour still held in absolute possession.

Mrs. Mount did not come out much; but there was a deferential manner in the bearing of the men toward her, which those haughty creatures accord not save to clever women; and she contrived to hold the talk with three or four at the head of the table while she still had passages aside with Richard.

The port and claret went very well after the champagne. The ladies here did not ignominiously surrender the field to the gentlemen; they maintained their position with honour. Silver was seen far out on Thames. The wine ebbed, and the laughter. Sentiment and cigars took up the wondrous tale.

"Oh, what a lovely night!" said the ladies, looking above.

"Charming," said the gentlemen, looking below.

> The faint-smelling cool Autumn air was pleasant after
> the feast.
> Fragrant weeds burned bright about the garden.

"We are split into couples," said Adrian to Richard, who was standing alone, eying the landscape. "Tis the influence of the moon! Apparently we are in Cyprus. How has my son enjoyed himself? How likes he the society of Aspasia? I feel like a wise Greek to-night."

Adrian was jolly, and rolled comfortably as he talked. Ripton had been carried off by the sentimental bosom. He came up to them and whispered: "By Jove, Ricky! do you know what sort of women these are?"

Richard said he thought them a nice sort.

"Puritan!" exclaimed Adrian, slapping Ripton on the back. "Why didn't you get tipsy, sir? Don't you ever intoxicate yourself except at lawful marriages? Reveal to us what you have done with the portly dame?"

Ripton endured his bantering that he might hang about Richard, and watch over him. He was jealous of his innocent Beauty's husband being in proximity with such women. Murmuring couples passed them to and fro.

"By Jove, Ricky!" Ripton favoured his friend with another hard whisper, "there's a woman smoking!"

"And why not, O Riptonus?" said Adrian. "Art unaware that woman cosmopolitan is woman consummate? and dost grumble to pay the small price for the splendid gem?"

"Well, I don't like women to smoke," said plain Ripton.

"Why mayn't they do what men do?" the hero cried impetuously. "I hate that contemptible narrow-mindedness. It's that makes the ruin and horrors I see. Why mayn't they do what men do? I like the women who are brave enough not to be hypocrites. By heaven! if these women are bad,

I like them better than a set of hypocritical creatures who are all show, and deceive you in the end."

"Bravo!" shouted Adrian. "There speaks the regenerator."

Ripton, as usual, was crushed by his leader. He had no argument. He still thought women ought not to smoke; and he thought of one far away, lonely by the sea, who was perfect without being cosmopolitan.

The Pilgrim's Scrip remarks that: "Young men take joy in nothing so much as the thinking women Angels: and nothing sours men of experience more than knowing that all are not quite so."

The Aphorist would have pardoned Ripton Thompson his first Random extravagance, had he perceived the simple warm-hearted worship of feminine goodness Richard's young bride had inspired in the breast of the youth. It might possibly have taught him to put deeper trust in our nature.

Ripton thought of her, and had a feeling of sadness. He wandered about the grounds by himself, went through an open postern, and threw himself down among some bushes on the slope of the hill. Lying there, and meditating, he became aware of voices conversing.

"What does he want?" said a woman's voice. "It's another of his villanies, I know. Upon my honour, Brayder, when I think of what I have to reproach him for, I think I must go mad, or kill him."

"Tragic!" said the Hon. Peter. "Haven't you revenged yourself, Bella, pretty often? Best deal openly. This is a commercial transaction. You ask for money, and you are to have it—on the conditions: double the sum, and debts paid."

"He applies to me!"

"You know, my dear Bella, it has long been all up between you. I think Mount has behaved very well, considering all he knows. He's not easily hoodwinked, you know. He resigns himself to his fate and follows other game."

"Then the condition is, that I am to seduce this young man?"

"My dear Bella! you strike your bird like a hawk. I didn't say seduce.
Hold him in—play with him. Amuse him."

"I don't understand half-measures."

"Women seldom do."

"How I hate you, Brayder!"

"I thank your ladyship."

The two walked farther. Ripton had heard some little of the colloquy. He left the spot in a serious mood, apprehensive of something dark to the people he loved, though he had no idea of what the Hon. Peter's stipulation involved.

On the voyage back to town, Richard was again selected to sit by Mrs. Mount. Brayder and Adrian started the jokes. The pair of parasites got on extremely well together. Soft fell the plash of the oars; softly the moonlight curled around them; softly the banks glided by. The ladies were in a state of high sentiment. They sang without request. All deemed the British ballad-monger an appropriate interpreter of their emotions. After good wine, and plenty thereof, fair throats will make men of taste swallow that remarkable composer. Eyes, lips, hearts; darts and smarts and sighs; beauty, duty; bosom, blossom; false one, farewell! To this pathetic strain they melted. Mrs. Mount, though strongly requested, declined to sing. She preserved her state. Under the tall aspens of Brentford-ait, and on they swept, the white moon in their wake. Richard's hand lay open by his side. Mrs. Mount's little white hand by misadventure fell into it. It was not pressed, or soothed for its fall, or made intimate with eloquent fingers. It lay there like a bit of snow on the cold ground. A yellow leaf wavering down from the aspens struck Richard's cheek, and he drew away the very hand to throw back his hair and smooth his face, and then folded his arms, unconscious of offence. He was thinking ambitiously of his life: his blood was untroubled, his brain calmly working.

"Which is the more perilous?" is a problem put by the Pilgrim: "To meet the temptings of Eve, or to pique her?"

Mrs. Mount stared at the young man as at a curiosity, and turned to flirt with one of her Court. The Guardsmen were mostly sentimental. One or two rattled, and one was such a good-humoured fellow that Adrian could not make him ridiculous. The others seemed to give themselves up to a silent waxing in length of limb. However far they sat removed, everybody was entangled in their legs. Pursuing his studies, Adrian came to the conclusion, that the same close intellectual and moral affinity which he had discovered to exist between our nobility and our yeomanry, is to be observed between the Guardsman class, and that of the corps de ballet: they both live by the strength of their legs, where also their wits, if they do not altogether reside there, are principally developed: both are volage; wine, tobacco, and the moon, influence both alike; and admitting the one marked difference that does exist, it is, after all, pretty nearly the same thing to be coquetting and sinning on two legs as on the point of a toe.

A long Guardsman with a deep bass voice sang a doleful song about the twining tendrils of the heart ruthlessly torn, but required urgent persuasions and heavy trumpeting of his lungs to get to the end: before he had accomplished it, Adrian had contrived to raise a laugh in his neighbourhood, so that the company was divided, and the camp split: jollity returned to one-half, while sentiment held the other. Ripton, blotted behind the bosom, was only lucky in securing a higher degree of heat than was possible for the rest. "Are you cold?" she would ask, smiling charitably.

"I am," said the mignonne, as if to excuse her conduct.

"You always appear to be," the fat one sniffed and snapped.

"Won't you warm two, Mrs. Mortimer?" said the naughty little woman.

Disdain prevented any further notice of her. Those familiar with the ladies enjoyed their sparring, which was frequent. The mignonne was heard to whisper: "That poor fellow will certainly be stewed."

Very prettily the ladies took and gave warmth, for the air on the water was chill and misty. Adrian had beside him the demure one who had stopped the circulation of his anecdote. She in nowise objected to the fair exchange, but said "Hush!" betweenwhiles.

Past Kew and Hammersmith, on the cool smooth water; across Putney reach; through Battersea bridge; and the City grew around them, and the shadows of great mill-factories slept athwart the moonlight.

All the ladies prattled sweetly of a charming day when they alighted on land. Several cavaliers crushed for the honour of conducting Mrs. Mount to her home.

"My brougham's here; I shall go alone," said Mrs. Mount. "Some one arrange my shawl."

She turned her back to Richard, who had a view of a delicate neck as he manipulated with the bearing of a mailed knight.

"Which way are you going?" she asked carelessly, and, to his reply as to the direction, said: "Then I can give you a lift," and she took his arm with a matter-of-course air, and walked up the stairs with him.

Ripton saw what had happened. He was going to follow: the portly dame retained him, and desired him to get her a cab.

"Oh, you happy fellow!" said the bright-eyed mignonne, passing by.

Ripton procured the cab, and stuffed it full without having to get into it himself.

"Try and let him come in too?" said the persecuting creature, again passing.

"Take liberties with pour men—you shan't with me," retorted the angry bosom, and drove off.

"So she's been and gone and run away and left him after all his trouble!" cried the pert little thing, peering into Ripton's eyes. "Now you'll never be so foolish as to pin your faith to fat women again. There! he shall be made happy another time." She gave his nose a comical tap, and tripped away with her possessor.

Ripton rather forgot his friend for some minutes: Random thoughts laid hold of him. Cabs and carriages rattled past. He was sure he had been among members of the nobility that day, though when they went by him now they only recognized him with an effort of the eyelids. He began to think of the day with exultation, as an event. Recollections of the mignonne were captivating. "Blue eyes—just what I like! And such a little impudent nose, and red lips, pouting—the very thing I like! And her hair? darkish, I think—say brown. And so saucy, and light on her feet. And kind she is, or she wouldn't have talked to me like that." Thus, with a groaning soul, he pictured her. His reason voluntarily consigned her to the aristocracy as a natural appanage: but he did amorously wish that Fortune had made a lord of him.

Then his mind reverted to Mrs. Mount, and the strange bits of the conversation he had heard on the hill. He was not one to suspect anybody positively. He was timid of fixing a suspicion. It hovered indefinitely, and clouded people, without stirring him to any resolve. Still the attentions of the lady toward Richard were queer. He endeavoured to imagine they were in the nature of things, because Richard was so handsome that any woman must take to him. "But he's married," said Ripton, "and he mustn't go near these people if he's married." Not a high morality, perhaps better than none at all: better for the world were it practised more. He thought of Richard along with that sparkling dame, alone with her. The adorable beauty of his dear bride, her pure heavenly face, swam before him. Thinking of her, he lost sight of the mignonne who had made him giddy.

He walked to Richard's hotel, and up and down the street there, hoping every minute to hear his step; sometimes fancying he might have returned and gone to bed. Two o'clock struck. Ripton could not go away. He was sure he should not sleep if he did. At last the cold sent him homeward, and leaving the street, on the moonlight side of Piccadilly he met his friend patrolling with his head up and that swing of the feet proper to men who are chanting verses.

"Old Rip!" cried Richard, cheerily. "What on earth are you doing here at this hour of the morning?"

Ripton muttered of his pleasure at meeting him. "I wanted to shake your hand before I went home."

Richard smiled on him in an amused kindly way. "That all? You may shake my hand any day, like a true man as you are, old Rip! I've been speaking about you. Do you know, that—Mrs. Mount—never saw you all the time at Richmond, or in the boat!"

"Oh!" Ripton said, well assured that he was a dwarf "you saw her safe home?"

"Yes. I've been there for the last couple of hours—talking. She talks capitally: she's wonderfully clever. She's very like a man, only much nicer. I like her."

"But, Richard, excuse me—I'm sure I don't mean to offend you—but now you're married...perhaps you couldn't help seeing her home, but I think you really indeed oughtn't to have gone upstairs."

Ripton delivered this opinion with a modest impressiveness.

"What do you mean?" said Richard. "You don't suppose I care for any woman but my little darling down there." He laughed.

"No; of course not. That's absurd. What I mean is, that people perhaps will—you know, they do—they say all manner of things, and that makes unhappiness; and I do wish you were going home to-morrow, Ricky. I mean, to your dear wife." Ripton blushed and looked away as he spoke.

The hero gave one of his scornful glances. "So you're anxious about my reputation. I hate that way of looking on women. Because they have been once misled—look how much weaker they are!—because the world has given them an ill fame, you would treat them as contagious and keep away from them for the sake of your character!

"It would be different with me," quoth Ripton.

"How?" asked the hero.

"Because I'm worse than you," was all the logical explanation Ripton was capable of.

"I do hope you will go home soon," he added.

"Yes," said Richard, "and I, so do I hope so. But I've work to do now. I dare not, I cannot, leave it. Lucy would be the last to ask me;—you saw her letter yesterday. Now listen to me, Rip. I want to make you be just to women."

Then he read Ripton a lecture on erring women, speaking of them as if he had known them and studied them for years. Clever, beautiful, but betrayed by love, it was the first duty of all true men to cherish and redeem them. "We turn them into curses, Rip; these divine creatures." And the world suffered for it. That—that was the root of all the evil in the world!

"I don't feel anger or horror at these poor women, Rip! It's strange. I knew what they were when we came home in the boat. But I do—it tears my heart to see a young girl given over to an old man—a man she doesn't love. That's shame!—Don't speak of it."

Forgetting to contest the premiss, that all betrayed women are betrayed by love, Ripton was quite silenced. He, like most young men, had pondered somewhat on this matter, and was inclined to be sentimental when be was not hungry. They walked in the moonlight by the railings of the park. Richard harangued at leisure, while Ripton's teeth chattered. Chivalry might be dead, but still there was something to do, went the strain. The lady of the day had not been thrown in the hero's path without an object, he said; and he was sadly right there. He did not express the thing clearly; nevertheless Ripton understood him to mean, he intended to rescue that lady from further transgressions, and show a certain scorn of the world. That lady, and then other ladies unknown, were to be rescued. Ripton was to help. He and Ripton were to be the knights of this enterprise. When appealed to, Ripton acquiesced, and shivered. Not only were they to be knights, they would have to be Titans, for the powers of the world, the spurious ruling Social Gods, would have to be defied and overthrown. And Titan number one flung up his handsome bold face as if to challenge base Jove on the spot; and Titan number two strained the upper button of his coat to meet across his pocket-handkerchief on his chest, and warmed his fingers under his coat- tails. The moon had fallen from her high seat and was in the mists of the West, when he was allowed to seek his blankets, and the cold acting on his friend's eloquence made Ripton's flesh very contrite. The poor fellow had thinner blood than the hero; but his heart was good. By the time he had got a little warmth about him, his heart gratefully strove to encourage him in the conception of becoming a knight and a Titan; and so striving Ripton fell asleep and dreamed.

CHAPTER XXXVII

Behold the hero embarked in the redemption of an erring beautiful woman.

"Alas!" writes the Pilgrim at this very time to Lady Blandish, "I cannot get that legend of the Serpent from me, the more I think. Has he not caught you, and ranked you foremost in his legions? For see: till you were fashioned, the fruits hung immobile on the boughs. They swayed before us, glistening and cold. The hand must be eager that plucked them. They did not come down to us, and smile, and speak our language, and read our thoughts, and know when to fly, when to follow! how surely to have us!

"Do but mark one of you standing openly in the track of the Serpent. What shall be done with her? I fear the world is wiser than its judges! Turn from her, says the world. By day the sons of the world do. It darkens, and they dance together downward. Then comes there one of the world's elect who deems old counsel devilish; indifference to the end of evil worse than its pursuit. He comes to reclaim her. From deepest bane will he bring her back to highest blessing. Is not that a bait already? Poor fish! 'tis wondrous flattering. The Serpent has slimed her so to secure him! With slow weary steps he draws her into light: she clings to him; she is human; part of his work, and he loves it. As they mount upward, he looks on her more, while she, it may be, looks above. What has touched him? What has passed out of her, and into him? The Serpent laughs below. At the gateways of the Sun they fall together!"

This alliterative production was written without any sense of the peril that makes prophecy.

It suited Sir Austin to write thus. It was a channel to his acrimony moderated through his philosophy. The letter was a reply to a vehement entreaty from Lady Blandish for him to come up to Richard and forgive him thoroughly: Richard's name was not mentioned in it.

"He tries to be more than he is," thought the lady: and she began insensibly to conceive him less than he was.

The baronet was conscious of a certain false gratification in his son's apparent obedience to his wishes and complete submission; a gratification he chose to accept as his due, without dissecting or accounting for it. The intelligence reiterating that Richard waited, and still waited; Richard's letters, and more his dumb abiding and practical penitence; vindicated humanity sufficiently to stop the course of virulent aphorisms. He could speak, we have seen, in sorrow for this frail nature of ours, that he had once stood forth to champion. "But how long will this last?" he demanded, with the air of Hippias. He did not reflect how long it had lasted. Indeed, his indigestion of wrath had made of him a moral Dyspepsy.

It was not mere obedience that held Richard from the aims of his young wife: nor was it this new knightly enterprise he had presumed to undertake. Hero as he was, a youth, open to the insane promptings of hot blood, he was not a fool. There had been talk between him and Mrs. Doria of his mother. Now that he had broken from his father, his heart spoke for her. She lived, he knew: he knew no more. Words painfully hovering along the borders of plain speech had been communicated to him, filling him with moody imaginings. If he thought of her, the red was on his face, though he could not have said why. But now, after canvassing the conduct of his father, and throwing him aside as a terrible riddle, he asked Mrs. Doria to tell him of his other parent. As softly as she could she told the story. To her the shame was past: she could weep for the poor lady. Richard dropped no tears. Disgrace of this kind is always present to a son, and, educated as he had been, these tidings were a vivid fire in his brain. He resolved to hunt her out, and take her from the man. Here was work set to his hand. All her dear husband did was right to Lucy. She encouraged him to stay for that purpose, thinking it also served another. There was Tom Bakewell to watch over Lucy: there was work for him to do. Whether it would please his father he did not stop to consider. As to the justice of the act, let us say nothing.

On Ripton devolved the humbler task of grubbing for Sandoe's place of residence; and as he was unacquainted with the name by which the poet now went in private, his endeavours were not immediately successful. The friends met in the evening at Lady Blandish's town-house, or at the Foreys', where Mrs. Doria procured the reverer of the Royal Martyr, and staunch conservative, a favourable reception. Pity, deep pity for Richard's conduct Ripton saw breathing out of Mrs. Doria. Algernon Feverel treated his nephew with a sort of rough commiseration, as a young fellow who had run off the road.

Pity was in Lady Blandish's eyes, though for a different cause. She doubted if she did well in seconding his father's unwise scheme—supposing him to have a scheme. She saw the young husband encompassed by dangers at a critical time. Not a word of Mrs. Mount had been breathed to her, but the lady had some knowledge of life. She touched on delicate verges to the baronet in her letters, and he understood her well enough. "If he loves this person to whom he has bound himself, what fear for him? Or are you coming to think it something that bears the name of love because we have to veil the rightful appellation?" So he responded, remote among the mountains. She tried very hard to speak plainly. Finally he came to say that he denied himself the pleasure of seeing his son specially, that he for a time might be put to the test the lady seemed to dread. This was almost too much for Lady Blandish. Love's charity boy so loftily serene now that she saw him half denuded—a thing of shanks and wrists—was a trial for her true heart.

Going home at night Richard would laugh at the faces made about his marriage. "We'll carry the day, Rip, my Lucy and I! or I'll do it alone- -what there is to do." He slightly adverted to a natural want of courage in women, which Ripton took to indicate that his Beauty was deficient in that quality. Up leapt the Old Dog; "I'm sure there never was a braver creature upon earth, Richard! She's as brave as she's lovely, I'll swear she is! Look how she behaved that day! How her voice sounded! She was trembling... Brave? She'd follow you into battle, Richard!"

And Richard rejoined: "Talk on, dear old Rip! She's my darling love, whatever she is! And she is gloriously lovely. No eyes are like hers. I'll go down to-morrow morning the first thing."

Ripton only wondered the husband of such a treasure could remain apart from it. So thought Richard for a space.

"But if I go, Rip," he said despondently, "if I go for a day even I shall have undone all my work with my father. She says it herself—you saw it in her last letter."

> "Yes," Ripton assented, and the words "Please remember me to dear Mr. Thompson," fluttered about the Old Dog's heart.

It came to pass that Mrs. Berry, having certain business that led her through Kensington Gardens, spied a figure that she had once dandled in long clothes, and helped make a man of, if ever woman did. He was walking under the trees beside a lady, talking to her, not indifferently. The gentleman was her bridegroom and her babe. "I know his back," said Mrs. Berry, as if she had branded a mark on it in infancy. But the lady was not her bride. Mrs. Berry diverged from the path, and got before them on the left flank; she stared, retreated, and came round upon the right. There was that in the lady's face which Mrs. Berry did not like. Her innermost question was, why he was not walking with his own wife? She stopped in front of them. They broke, and passed about her. The lady made a laughing remark to him, whereat he turned to look, and Mrs. Berry bobbed. She had to bob a second time, and then he remembered the worthy creature, and hailed her Penelope, shaking her hand so that he put her in countenance again. Mrs. Berry was extremely agitated. He dismissed her, promising to call upon her in the evening. She heard the lady slip out something from a side of her lip, and they both laughed as she toddled off to a sheltering tree to wipe a corner of each eye. "I don't like the looks of that woman," she said, and repeated it resolutely.

"Why doesn't he walk arm-in-arm with her?" was her neat inquiry. "Where's his wife?" succeeded it. After many interrogations of the sort, she arrived at naming the lady a bold-faced thing; adding subsequently, brazen. The lady had apparently shown Mrs. Berry that she wished to get rid of her, and had checked the outpouring of her emotions on the breast of her babe. "I know a lady when I see one," said Mrs. Berry. "I haven't lived with 'em for nothing; and if she's a lady bred and born, I wasn't married in the church alive."

Then, if not a lady, what was she? Mrs. Berry desired to know: "She's imitation lady, I'm sure she is!" Berry vowed. "I say she don't look proper."

Establishing the lady to be a spurious article, however, what was one to think of a married man in company with such? "Oh no! it ain't that!" Mrs. Berry returned immediately on the charitable tack. "Belike it's some one of his acquaintance 've married her for her looks, and he've just met her.... Why it'd be as bad as my Berry!" the relinquished spouse of Berry ejaculated, in horror at the idea of a second man being so monstrous in wickedness. "Just coupled, too!" Mrs. Berry groaned on the suspicious side of the debate. "And such a sweet young thing for his wife! But no, I'll never believe it. Not if he tell me so himself! And men don't do that," she whimpered.

Women are swift at coming to conclusions in these matters; soft women exceedingly swift: and soft women who have been betrayed are rapid beyond measure. Mrs. Berry had not cogitated long ere she pronounced distinctly and without a shadow of dubiosity: "My opinion is—married or not married, and wheresomever he pick her up—she's nothin' more nor less than a Bella Donna!" as which poisonous plant she forthwith registered the lady in the botanical note-book of her brain. It would have astonished Mrs. Mount to have heard her person so accurately hit off at a glance.

In the evening Richard made good his promise, accompanied by Ripton. Mrs. Berry opened the door to them. She could not wait to get him into the parlour. "You're my own blessed babe; and I'm as good as your mother, though I didn't suck ye, bein' a maid!" she cried, falling into his arms, while Richard did his best to support the unexpected burden. Then reproaching him tenderly for his guile—at mention of which Ripton chuckled, deeming it his own most honourable portion of the plot—Mrs. Berry led them into the parlour, and revealed to Richard who she was, and how she had tossed him, and hugged him, and kissed him all over, when he was only that big—

showing him her stumpy fat arm. "I kissed ye from head to tail, I did," said Mrs. Berry, "and you needn't be ashamed of it. It's be hoped you'll never have nothin' worse come t'ye, my dear!"

Richard assured her he was not a bit ashamed, but warned her that she must not do it now, Mrs. Berry admitting it was out of the question now, and now that he had a wife, moreover. The young men laughed, and Ripton laughing over-loudly drew on himself Mrs. Berry's attention: "But that Mr. Thompson there—however he can look me in the face after his inn'cence! helping blindfold an old woman! though I ain't sorry for what I did—that I'm free for to say, and its' over, and blessed be all! Amen! So now where is she and how is she, Mr. Richard, my dear—it's only cuttin' off the 's' and you are as you was.—Why didn't ye bring her with ye to see her old Berry?"

Richard hurriedly explained that Lucy was still in the Isle of Wight.

"Oh! and you've left her for a day or two?" said Mrs. Berry.

"Good God! I wish it had been a day or two," cried Richard.

"Ah! and how long have it been?" asked Mrs. Berry, her heart beginning to beat at his manner of speaking.

"Don't talk about it," said Richard.

"Oh! you never been dudgeonin' already? Oh! you haven't been peckin' at one another yet?" Mrs. Berry exclaimed.

Ripton interposed to tell her such fears were unfounded.

"Then how long ha' you been divided?"

In a guilty voice Ripton stammered "since September."

"September!" breathed Mrs. Berry, counting on her fingers, "September, October, Nov—two months and more! nigh three! A young married husband away from the wife of his bosom nigh three months! Oh my! Oh my! what do that mean?"

"My father sent for me—I'm waiting to see him," said Richard. A few more words helped Mrs. Berry to comprehend the condition of affairs. Then Mrs. Berry spread her lap, flattened out her hands, fixed her eyes, and spoke.

"My dear young gentleman!—I'd like to call ye my darlin' babe! I'm going to speak as a mother to ye, whether ye likes it or no; and what old Berry says, you won't mind, for she's had ye when there was no conventionals about ye, and she has the feelin's of a mother to you, though humble her state. If there's one that know matrimony it's me, my dear, though Berry did give me no more but nine months of it and I've known the worst of matrimony, which, if you wants to be woeful wise, there it is for ye. For what have been my gain? That man gave me nothin' but his name; and

Bessy Andrews was as good as Bessy Berry, though both is 'Bs,' and says he, you was 'A,' and now you's 'B,' so you're my A B, he says, write yourself down that, he says, the bad man, with his jokes!—Berry went to service." Mrs. Berry's softness came upon her. "So I tell ye, Berry went to service. He left the wife of his bosom forlorn and he went to service; because he were allays an ambitious man, and wasn't, so to speak, happy out of his uniform—which was his livery—not even in my arms: and he let me know it. He got among them kitchen sluts, which was my mournin' ready made, and worse than a widow's cap to me, which is no shame to wear, and some say becoming. There's no man as ever lived known better than my Berry how to show his legs to advantage, and gals look at 'em. I don't wonder now that Berry was prostrated. His temptations was strong, and his flesh was weak. Then what I say is, that for a young married man—be he whomsoever he may be— to be separated from the wife of his bosom—a young sweet thing, and he an innocent young gentleman!—so to sunder, in their state, and be kep' from each other, I say it's as bad as bad can be! For what is matrimony, my dears? We're told it's a holy Ordnance. And why are ye so comfortable in matrimony? For that ye are not a sinnin'! And they that severs ye they tempts ye to stray: and you learn too late the meanin' o' them blessin's of the priest—as it was ordained. Separate—what comes? Fust it's like the circulation of your blood a-stoppin'—all goes wrong. Then there's misunderstandings—ye've both lost the key. Then, behold ye, there's birds o' prey hoverin' over each on ye, and it's which'll be snapped up fust. Then—Oh, dear! Oh, dear! it be like the devil come into the world again." Mrs. Berry struck her hands and moaned. "A day I'll give ye: I'll go so far as a week: but there's the outside. Three months dwellin' apart! That's not matrimony, it's divorcin'! what can it be to her but widowhood? widowhood with no cap to show for it! And what can it be to you, my dear? Think! you been a bachelor three months! and a bachelor man," Mrs. Berry shook her head most dolefully, "he ain't widow woman. I don't go to compare you to Berry, my dear young gentleman. Some men's hearts is vagabonds born— they must go astray— it's their natur' to. But all men are men, and I know the foundation of 'em, by reason of my woe."

Mrs. Berry paused. Richard was humorously respectful to the sermon. The truth in the good creature's address was not to be disputed, or despised, notwithstanding the inclination to laugh provoked by her quaint way of putting it. Ripton nodded encouragingly at every sentence, for he saw her drift, and wished to second it.

Seeking for an illustration of her meaning, Mrs. Berry solemnly continued: "We all know what checked prespiration is." But neither of the young gentlemen could resist this. Out they burst in a roar of laughter.

"Laugh away," said Mrs. Berry. "I don't mind ye. I say again, we all do know what checked prespiration is. It fly to the lungs, it gives ye mortal inflammation, and it carries ye off. Then I say checked matrimony is as bad. It fly to the heart, and it carries off the virtue that's in ye, and you might as well be dead! Them that is joined it's their salvation not to separate! It don't so much matter before it. That Mr. Thompson there—if he go astray, it ain't from the blessed fold. He hurt himself alone—not double, and belike treble, for who can say now what may be? There's time for it. I'm for holding back young people so that they knows their minds, howsomever they rattles about their hearts. I ain't a speeder of matrimony, and good's my reason! but where it's been done—where they're lawfully joined, and their bodies made one, I do say this, that to put division between 'em then, it's to make wanderin' comets of 'em—creatures without a objeck, and no soul can say what they's good for but to rush about!"

Mrs. Berry here took a heavy breath, as one who has said her utmost for the time being.

"My dear old girl," Richard went up to her and, applauding her on the shoulder, "you're a very wise old woman. But you mustn't speak to me as if I wanted to stop here. I'm compelled to. I do it for her good chiefly."

"It's your father that's doin' it, my dear?"

"Well, I'm waiting his pleasure."

> "A pretty pleasure! puttin' a snake in the nest of young
> turtle-doves!
> And why don't she come up to you?"

"Well, that you must ask her. The fact is, she's a little timid girl— she wants me to see him first, and when I've made all right, then she'll come."

"A little timid girl!" cried Mrs. Berry. "Oh, lor', how she must ha' deceived ye to make ye think that! Look at that ring," she held out her finger, "he's a stranger: he's not my lawful! You know what ye did to me, my dear. Could I get my own wedding-ring back from her? "No!" says she, firm as a rock, 'he said, with this ring I thee wed'—I think I see her now, with her pretty eyes and lovesome locks—a darlin'!—And that ring she'd keep to, come life, came death. And she must ha' been a rock for me to give in to her in that. For what's the consequence? Here am I," Mrs. Berry smoothed down the back of her hand mournfully, "here am I in a strange ring, that's like a strange man holdin' of me, and me a- wearin' of it just to seem decent, and feelin' all over no better than a b—a big—that nasty came I can't abide!—I tell you, my dear, she ain't soft, no!—except to the man of her heart; and the best of women's too soft there—mores our sorrow!"

"Well, well!" said Richard, who thought he knew.

"I agree with you, Mrs. Berry," Ripton struck in, "Mrs. Richard would do anything in the world her husband asked her, I'm quite sure."

"Bless you for your good opinion, Mr. Thompson! Why, see her! she ain't frail on her feet; she looks ye straight in the eyes; she ain't one of your hang-down misses. Look how she behaved at the ceremony!"

"Ah!" sighed Ripton.

"And if you'd ha' seen her when she spoke to me about my ring! Depend upon it, my dear Mr. Richard, if she blinded you about the nerve she've got, it was somethin' she thought she ought to do for your sake, and I wish I'd been by to counsel her, poor blessed babe!—And how much longer, now, can ye stay divided from that darlin'?"

Richard paced up and down.

"A father's will," urged Mrs. Berry, "that's a son's law; but he mustn't go again' the laws of his nature to do it."

"Just be quiet at present—talk of other things, there's a good woman," said Richard.

Mrs. Berry meekly folded her arms.

"How strange, now, our meetin' like this! meetin' at all, too!" she remarked contemplatively. "It's them advertisements! They brings people together from the ends of the earth, for good or for bad. I often say, there's more lucky accidents, or unlucky ones, since advertisements was the rule, than ever there was before. They make a number of romances, depend upon it! Do you walk much in the Gardens, my dear?"

"Now and then," said Richard.

"Very pleasant it is there with the fine folks and flowers and titled people," continued Mrs. Berry. "That was a handsome woman you was a-walkin' beside, this mornin'."

Very," said Richard.

"She was a handsome woman! or I should say, is, for her day ain't past, and she know it. I thought at first—by her back—it might ha' been your aunt, Mrs. Forey; for she do step out well and hold up her shoulders: straight as a dart she be! But when I come to see her face—Oh, dear me! says I, this ain't one of the family. They none of 'em got such bold faces—nor no lady as I know have. But she's a fine woman—that nobody can gainsay."

Mrs. Berry talked further of the fine woman. It was a liberty she took to speak in this disrespectful tone of her, and Mrs. Berry was quite aware that she was laying herself open to rebuke. She had her end in view. No rebuke was uttered, and during her talk she observed intercourse passing between the eyes of the young men.

"Look here, Penelope," Richard stopped her at last. "Will it make you comfortable if I tell you I'll obey the laws of my nature and go down at the end of the week?"

"I'll thank the Lord of heaven if you do!" she exclaimed.

"Very well, then—be happy—I will. Now listen. I want you to keep your rooms for me—those she had. I expect, in a day or two, to bring a lady here"—

"A lady?" faltered Mrs. Berry.

"Yes. A lady."

"May I make so bold as to ask what lady?"

"You may not. Not now. Of course you will know."

Mrs. Berry's short neck made the best imitation it could of an offended swan's action. She was very angry. She said she did not like so many ladies, which natural objection Richard met by saying that there was only one lady.

"And Mrs. Berry," he added, dropping his voice. "You will treat her as you did my dear girl, for she will require not only shelter but kindness. I would rather leave her with you than with any one. She has been very unfortunate."

His serious air and habitual tone of command fascinated the softness of Berry, and it was not until he had gone that she spoke out. "Unfort'nate! He's going to bring me an unfort'nate female! Oh! not from my babe can I bear that! Never will I have her here! I see it. It's that bold-faced woman he's got mixed up in, and she've been and made the young man think he'll go for to reform her. It's one o' their arts— that is; and he's too innocent a young man to mean anythin' else. But I ain't a house of Magdalens no! and sooner than have her here I'd have the roof fall over me, I would."

She sat down to eat her supper on the sublime resolve.

In love, Mrs. Berry's charity was all on the side of the law, and this is the case with many of her sisters. The Pilgrim sneers at them for it, and would have us credit that it is their admirable instinct which, at the expense of every virtue save one, preserves the artificial barrier simply to impose upon us. Men, I presume, are hardly fair judges, and should stand aside and mark.

Early next day Mrs. Berry bundled off to Richard's hotel to let him know her determination. She did not find him there. Returning homeward through the park, she beheld him on horseback riding by the side of the identical lady.

The sight of this public exposure shocked her more than the secret walk under the trees... "You don't look near your reform yet," Mrs. Berry apostrophized her. "You don't look to me one that'd come the Fair Penitent till you've left off bein' fair—if then you do, which some of ye don't. Laugh away and show yet airs! Spite o' your hat and feather, and your ridin' habit, you're a Belle Donna." Setting her down again absolutely for such, whatever it might signify, Mrs. Berry had a virtuous glow.

In the evening she heard the noise of wheels stopping at the door. "Never!" she rose from her chair to exclaim. "He ain't rided her out in the mornin', and been and made a Magdalen of her afore dark?"

A lady veiled was brought into the house by Richard. Mrs. Berry feebly tried to bar his progress in the passage. He pushed past her, and conducted the lady into the parlour without speaking. Mrs. Berry did not follow. She heard him murmur a few sentences within. Then he came out. All her crest stood up, as she whispered vigorously, "Mr. Richard! if that woman stay here, I go forth. My house ain't a penitentiary for unfort'nate females, sir"—

He frowned at her curiously; but as she was on the point of renewing her indignant protest, he clapped his hand across her mouth, and spoke words in her ear that had awful import to her. She trembled, breathing low: "My God, forgive, me!

"Richard?" And her virtue was humbled. "Lady Feverel is it? Your mother, Mr. Richard?" And her virtue was humbled.

CHAPTER XXXVIII

One may suppose that a prematurely aged, oily little man; a poet in bad circumstances; a decrepit butterfly chained to a disappointed inkstand, will not put out strenuous energies to retain his ancient paramour when a robust young man comes imperatively to demand his mother of him in her person. The colloquy was short between Diaper Sandoe and Richard. The question was referred to the poor spiritless lady, who, seeing that her son made no question of it, cast herself on his hands. Small loss to her was Diaper; but he was the loss of habit, and that is something to a woman who has lived. The blood of her son had been running so long alien from her that the sense of her motherhood smote he now with strangeness, and Richard's stern gentleness seemed like dreadful justice come upon her. Her heart had almost forgotten its maternal functions. She called him Sir, till he bade her remember he was her son. Her voice sounded to him like that of a broken-throated lamb, so painful and weak it was, with the plaintive stop in the utterance. When he kissed her, her skin was cold. Her thin hand fell out of his when his grasp related. "Can sin hunt one like this?" he asked, bitterly reproaching himself for the shame she had caused him to endure, and a deep compassion filled his breast.

Poetic justice had been dealt to Diaper the poet. He thought of all he had sacrificed for this woman—the comfortable quarters, the friend, the happy flights. He could not but accuse her of unfaithfulness in leaving him in his old age. Habit had legalized his union with her. He wrote as pathetically of the break of habit as men feel at the death of love, and when we are old and have no fair hope tossing golden locks before us, a wound to this our second nature is quite as sad. I know not even if it be not actually sadder.

Day by day Richard visited his mother. Lady Blandish and Ripton alone were in the secret. Adrian let him do as he pleased. He thought proper to tell him that the public recognition he accorded to a particular lady was, in the present state of the world, scarcely prudent.

"'Tis a proof to me of your moral rectitude, my son, but the world will not think so. No one character is sufficient to cover two—in a Protestant country especially. The divinity that doth hedge a Bishop would have no chance, in contact with your Madam Danae. Drop the woman, my son. Or permit me to speak what you would have her hear."

Richard listened to him with disgust. "Well, you've had my doctorial warning," said Adrian; and plunged back into his book.

When Lady Feverel had revived to take part in the consultations Mrs. Berry perpetually opened on the subject of Richard's matrimonial duty, another chain was cast about him. "Do not, oh, do not offend your father!" was her one repeated supplication. Sir Austin had grown to be a vindictive phantom in her mind. She never wept but when she said this.

So Mrs. Berry, to whom Richard had once made mention of Lady Blandish as the only friend he had among women, bundled off in her black-satin dress to obtain an interview with her, and an ally. After coming to an understanding on the matter of the visit, and reiterating many of her views concerning young married people, Mrs. Berry said: "My lady, if I may speak so bold, I'd say the sin that's bein' done is the sin o' the lookers-on. And when everybody appear frightened by that young gentleman's father, I'll say—hopin' your pardon—they no cause be frighted at all. For though it's nigh twenty year since I knew him, and I knew him then just sixteen months—no more—I'll say his heart's as soft as a woman's, which I've cause for to know. And that's it. That's where everybody's deceived by him, and I was. It's because he keeps his face, and makes ye think you're dealin' with a man of iron, and all the while there's a woman underneath. And a man that's like a woman he's the puzzle o' life! We can see through ourselves, my lady, and we can see through men, but one o' that sort—he's like somethin' out of nature. Then I say—hopin' be excused—what's to do is for to treat him like a woman, and not for to let him have his own way—which he don't know himself, and is why nobody else do. Let that sweet young couple come together, and be wholesome in spite of him, I say; and then give him time to come round, just like a woman; and round he'll come, and give 'em his blessin', and we shall know we've made him comfortable. He's angry because matrimony have come between him and his son, and he, woman-like, he's wantin' to treat what is as if it isn't. But matrimony's a holier than him. It began long long before him, and it's be hoped will endoor longs the time after, if the world's not coming to rack—wishin' him no harm."

Now Mrs. Berry only put Lady Blandish's thoughts in bad English. The lady took upon herself seriously to advise Richard to send for his wife. He wrote, bidding her come. Lucy, however, had wits, and inexperienced wits are as a little knowledge. In pursuance of her sage plan to make the family feel her worth, and to conquer the members of it one by one, she had got up a correspondence with Adrian, whom it tickled. Adrian constantly assured her all was going well: time would heal the wound if both the offenders had the fortitude to be patient: he fancied he saw signs of the baronet's relenting: they must do nothing to arrest those favourable symptoms. Indeed the wise youth was languidly seeking to produce them. He wrote, and felt, as Lucy's benefactor. So Lucy replied to her husband a cheerful rigmarole he could make nothing of, save that she was happy in hope, and still had fears. Then Mrs. Berry trained her fist to indite a letter to her bride. Her bride answered it by saying she trusted to time. "You poor marter" Mrs. Berry wrote back, "I know what your sufferin's be. They is the only kind a wife should never hide from her husband. He thinks all sorts of things if she can abide being away. And you trusting to time, why it's like trusting not to catch cold out of your natural clothes." There was no shaking Lucy's firmness.

Richard gave it up. He began to think that the life lying behind him was the life of a fool. What had he done in it? He had burnt a rick and got married! He associated the two acts of his existence. Where was the hero he was to have carved out of Tom Bakewell!—a wretch he had taught to lie and chicane: and for what? Great heavens! how ignoble did a flash from the light of his aspirations make his marriage appear! The young man sought amusement. He allowed his aunt to drag him into society, and sick of that he made late evening calls on Mrs. Mount, oblivious of the purpose he had in visiting her at all. Her man-like conversation, which he took for honesty, was a refreshing change on fair lips.

"Call me Bella: I'll call you Dick," said she. And it came to be Bella and Dick between them. No mention of Bella occurred in Richard's letters to Lucy.

Mrs. Mount spoke quite openly of herself. "I pretend to be no better than I am," she said, "and I know I'm no worse than many a woman who holds her head high." To back this she told him stories of blooming dames of good repute, and poured a little social sewerage into his ears.

Also she understood him. "What you want, my dear Dick, is something to do. You went and got married like a—hum!—friends must be respectful. Go into the Army. Try the turf. I can put you up to a trick or two— friends should make themselves useful."

She told him what she liked in him. "You're the only man I was ever alone with who don't talk to me of love and make me feel sick. I hate men who can't speak to a woman sensibly.—Just wait a minute." She left him and presently returned with, "Ah, Dick! old fellow! how are you?"— arrayed like a cavalier, one arm stuck in her side, her hat jauntily cocked, and a pretty oath on her lips to give reality to the costume. "What do you think of me? Wasn't it a shame to make a woman of me when I was born to be a man?"

"I don't know that," said Richard, for the contrast in her attire to those shooting eyes and lips, aired her sex bewitchingly.

"What! you think I don't do it well?"

"Charming! but I can't forget..."

"Now that is too bad!" she pouted.

Then she proposed that they should go out into the midnight streets arm- in-arm, and out they went and had great fits of laughter at her impertinent manner of using her eyeglass, and outrageous affectation of the supreme dandy.

"They take up men, Dick, for going about in women's clothes, and vice versaw, I suppose. You'll bail me, old fellaa, if I have to make my bow to the beak, won't you? Say it's becas I'm an honest woman and don't care to hide the—a—unmentionables when I wear them—as the t'others do," sprinkled with the dandy's famous invocations.

He began to conceive romance in that sort of fun.

"You're a wopper, my brave Dick! won't let any peeler take me? by Jove!"

And he with many assurances guaranteed to stand by her, while she bent her thin fingers trying the muscle of his arm; and reposed upon it more. There was delicacy in her dandyism. She was a graceful cavalier.

"Sir Julius," as they named the dandy's attire, was frequently called for on his evening visits to Mrs. Mount. When he beheld Sir Julius he thought of the lady, and "vice versaw," as Sir Julius was fond of exclaiming.

Was ever hero in this fashion wooed?

The woman now and then would peep through Sir Julius. Or she would sit, and talk, and altogether forget she was impersonating that worthy fop.

She never uttered an idea or a reflection, but Richard thought her the cleverest woman he had ever met.

All kinds of problematic notions beset him. She was cold as ice, she hated talk about love, and she was branded by the world.

A rumour spread that reached Mrs. Doria's ears. She rushed to Adrian first. The wise youth believed there was nothing in it. She sailed down upon Richard. "Is this true? that you have been seen going publicly about with an infamous woman, Richard? Tell me! pray, relieve me!"

Richard knew of no person answering to his aunt's description in whose company he could have been seen.

"Tell me, I say! Don't quibble. Do you know any woman of bad character?"

The acquaintance of a lady very much misjudged and
ill-used by the world,
Richard admitted to.

Urgent grave advice Mrs. Doria tendered her nephew, both from the moral and the worldly point of view, mentally ejaculating all the while: "That ridiculous System! That disgraceful marriage!" Sir Austin in his mountain solitude was furnished with serious stuff to brood over.

The rumour came to Lady Blandish. She likewise lectured Richard, and with her he condescended to argue. But he found himself obliged to instance something he had quite neglected. "Instead of her doing me harm, it's I that will do her good."

Lady Blandish shook her head and held up her finger. "This person must be very clever to have given you that delusion, dear."

"She is clever. And the world treats her shamefully."

"She complains of her position to you?"

"Not a word. But I will stand by her. She has no friend but me."

"My poor boy! has she made you think that?"

"How unjust you all are!" cried Richard.

"How mad and wicked is the man who can let him be
tempted so!" thought Lady Blandish.

He would pronounce no promise not to visit her, not to address her publicly. The world that condemned her and cast her out was no better—worse for its miserable hypocrisy. He knew the world now, the young man said.

"My child! the world may be very bad. I am not going to defend it. But you have some one else to think of. Have you forgotten you have a wife, Richard?"

"Ay! you all speak of her now. There's my aunt: 'Remember you have a wife!' "Do you think I love any one but Lucy? poor little thing! Because I am married am I to give up the society of women?"

"Of women!"

"Isn't she a woman?"

"Too much so!" sighed the defender of her sex.

Adrian became more emphatic in his warnings. Richard laughed at him. The wise youth sneered at Mrs. Mount. The hero then favoured him with a warning equal to his own in emphasis, and surpassing it in sincerity.

"We won't quarrel, my dear boy," said Adrian. "I'm a man of peace. Besides, we are not fairly proportioned for a combat. Ride your steed to virtue's goal! All I say is, that I think he'll upset you, and it's better to go at a slow pace and in companionship with the children of the sun. You have a very nice little woman for a wife—well, good-bye!"

To have his wife and the world thrown at his face, was unendurable to Richard; he associated them somewhat after the manner of the rick and the marriage. Charming Sir Julius, always gay, always honest, dispersed his black moods.

"Why, you're taller," Richard made the discovery.

"Of course I am. Don't you remember you said I was such a little thing when I came out of my woman's shell?"

"And how have you done it?"

"Grown to please you."

"Now, if you can do that, you can do anything."

"And so I would do anything."

"You would?"

"Honour!"

"Then"...his project recurred to him. But the incongruity of speaking seriously to Sir Julius struck him dumb.

"Then what?" asked she.

"Then you're a gallant fellow."

"That all?"

"Isn't it enough?"

"Not quite. You were going to say something. I saw it in your eyes."

"You saw that I admired you."

"Yes, but a man mustn't admire a man."

"I suppose I had an idea you were a woman."

"What! when I had the heels of my boots raised half an inch," Sir Julius turned one heel, and volleyed out silver laughter.

"I don't come much above your shoulder even now," she said, and proceeded to measure her height beside him with arch up-glances.

"You must grow more."

"'Fraid I can't, Dick! Bootmakers can't do it."

"I'll show you how," and he lifted Sir Julius lightly, and bore the fair gentleman to the looking-glass, holding him there exactly on a level with his head. "Will that do?"

"Yes! Oh but I can't stay here."

"Why can't you?"

"Why can't I?"

He should have known then—it was thundered at a closed door in him, that he played with fire. But the door being closed, he thought himself internally secure.

Their eyes met. He put her down instantly.

Sir Julius, charming as he was, lost his vogue. Seeing that, the wily woman resumed her shell. The memory, of Sir Julius breathing about her still, doubled the feminine attraction.

"I ought to have been an actress," she said.

Richard told her he found all natural women had a similar wish.

"Yes! Ah! then! if I had been!" sighed Mrs. Mount, gazing on the pattern of the carpet.

He took her hand, and pressed it.

"You are not happy as you are?"

"No."

"May I speak to you?"

"Yes."

Her nearest eye, setting a dimple of her cheek in motion, slid to the corner toward her ear, as she sat with her head sideways to him, listening. When he had gone, she said to herself: "Old hypocrites talk in that way; but I never heard of a young man doing it, and not making love at the same time."

Their next meeting displayed her quieter: subdued as one who had been set thinking. He lauded her fair looks.

"Don't make me thrice ashamed," she petitioned.

But it was not only that mood with her. Dauntless defiance, that splendidly befitted her gallant outline and gave a wildness to her bright bold eyes, when she would call out: "Happy? who dares say I'm not happy? D'you think if the world whips me I'll wince? D'you think I care for what they say or do? Let them kill me! they shall never get one cry out of me!" and flashing on the young man as if he were the congregated enemy, add:

"There! now you know me!"—that was a mood that well became her, and helped the work. She ought to have been an actress.

"This must not go on," said Lady Blandish and Mrs. Doria in unison. A common object brought them together. They confined their talk to it, and did not disagree. Mrs. Doria engaged to go down to the baronet. Both ladies knew it was a dangerous, likely to turn out a disastrous, expedition. They agreed to it because it was something to do, and doing anything is better than doing nothing. "Do it," said the wise youth, when they made him a third, "do it, if you want him to be a hermit for life. You will bring back nothing but his dead body, ladies—a Hellenic, rather than a Roman, triumph. He will listen to you—he will accompany you to the station—he will hand you into the carriage—and when you point to his seat he will bow profoundly, and retire into his congenial mists."

Adrian spoke their thoughts. They fretted; they relapsed.

"Speak to him, you, Adrian," said Mrs. Doria. "Speak to the boy solemnly. It would be almost better he should go back to that little thing he has married."

"Almost?" Lady Blandish opened her eyes. "I have been advising it for the last month and more."

"A choice of evils," said Mrs. Doria's sour-sweet face and shake of the head.

Each lady saw a point of dissension, and mutually agreed, with heroic effort, to avoid it by shutting their mouths. What was more, they preserved the peace in spite of Adrian's artifices.

"Well, I'll talk to him again," he said. "I'll try to get the Engine on the conventional line."

"Command him!" exclaimed Mrs. Doria.

> "Gentle means are, I think, the only means with Richard,"
> said Lady Blandish.

Throwing banter aside, as much as he could, Adrian spoke to Richard. "You want to reform this woman. Her manner is open—fair and free—the traditional characteristic. We won't stop to canvass how that particular honesty of deportment that wins your approbation has been gained. In her college it is not uncommon. Girls, you know, are not like boys. At a certain age they can't be quite natural. It's a bad sign if they don't blush, and fib, and affect this and that. It wears off when they're women. But a woman who speaks like a man, and has all those excellent virtues you admire—where has she learned the trick? She tells you. You don't surely approve of the school? Well, what is there in it, then? Reform her, of course. The task is worthy of your energies. But, if you are appointed to do it, don't do it publicly, and don't attempt it just now. May I ask you whether your wife participates in this undertaking?"

Richard walked away from the interrogation. The wise youth, who hated long unrelieved speeches and had healed his conscience, said no more.

Dear tender Lucy! Poor darling! Richard's eyes moistened. Her letters seemed sadder latterly. Yet she never called to him to come, or he would have gone. His heart leapt up to her. He announced to Adrian that he should wait no longer for his father. Adrian placidly nodded.

The enchantress observed that her knight had a clouded brow and an absent voice.

> "Richard—I can't call you Dick now, I really don't know
> why"—she said,
> "I want to beg a favour of you."

"Name it. I can still call you Bella, I suppose?"

"If you care to. What I want to say is this: when you meet me out—to cut it short—please not to recognize me."

"And why?"

"Do you ask to be told that?"

"Certainly I do."

"Then look: I won't compromise you."

"I see no harm, Bella."

"No," she caressed his hand, "and there is none. I know that. But," modest eyelids were drooped, "other people do," struggling eyes were raised.

"What do we care for other people?"

"Nothing. I don't. Not that!" snapping her finger, "I care for you, though." A prolonged look followed the declaration.

"You're foolish, Bella."

"Not quite so giddy—that's all."

He did not combat it with his usual impetuosity. Adrian's abrupt inquiry had sunk in his mind, as the wise youth intended it should. He had instinctively refrained from speaking to Lucy of this lady. But what a noble creature the woman was!

So they met in the park; Mrs. Mount whipped past him; and secresy added a new sense to their intimacy.

Adrian was gratified at the result produced by his eloquence.

Though this lady never expressed an idea, Richard was not mistaken in her cleverness. She could make evenings pass gaily, and one was not the fellow to the other. She could make you forget she was a woman, and then bring the fact startlingly home to you. She could read men with one quiver of her half-closed eye-lashes. She could catch the coming mood in a man, and fit herself to it. What does a woman want with ideas, who can do thus much? Keenness of perception, conformity, delicacy of handling, these be all the qualities necessary to parasites.

Love would have scared the youth: she banished it from her tongue. It may also have been true that it sickened her. She played on his higher nature. She understood spontaneously what would be most strange and taking to him in a woman. Various as the Serpent of old Nile, she acted fallen beauty, humorous indifference, reckless daring, arrogance in ruin. And acting thus, what think you?—She did it so well because she was growing half in earnest.

"Richard! I am not what I was since I knew you. You will not give me up quite?"

"Never, Bella."

"I am not so bad as I'm painted!"

"You are only unfortunate."

"Now that I know you I think so, and yet I am happier."

She told him her history when this soft horizon of repentance seemed to throw heaven's twilight across it. A woman's history, you know: certain chapters expunged. It was dark enough to Richard.

"Did you love the man?" he asked. "You say you love no one now."

"Did I love him? He was a nobleman and I a tradesman's daughter. No. I did not love him. I have lived to learn it. And now I should hate him, if I did not despise him."

"Can you be deceived in love?" said Richard, more to himself than to her.

"Yes. When we're young we can be very easily deceived. If there is such a thing as love, we discover it after we have tossed about and roughed it.

Then we find the man, or the woman, that suits us:—and then it's too late! we can't have him."

"Singular!" murmured Richard, "she says just what my father said."

He spoke aloud: "I could forgive you if you had loved him."

"Don't be harsh, grave judge! How is a girl to distinguish?"

"You had some affection for him? He was the first?"

She chose to admit that. "Yes. And the first who talks of love to a girl must be a fool if he doesn't blind her."

"That makes what is called first love nonsense."

"Isn't it?"

He repelled the insinuation. "Because I know it is not, Bella."

Nevertheless she had opened a wider view of the world to him, and a colder. He thought poorly of girls. A woman a sensible, brave, beautiful woman seemed, on comparison, infinitely nobler than those weak creatures.

She was best in her character of lovely rebel accusing foul injustice. "What am I to do? You tell me to be different. How can I? What am I to do? Will virtuous people let me earn my bread? I could not get a housemaid's place! They wouldn't have me—I see their noses smelling! Yes I can go to the hospital and sing behind a screen! Do you expect me to bury myself alive? Why, man, I have blood: I can't become a stone. You say I am honest, and I will be. Then let me till you that I have been used to luxuries, and I can't do without them. I might have married men—lots would have had me. But who marries one like me but a fool? and I could not marry a fool. The man I marry I must respect. He could not respect me—I should know him to be a fools and I should be worse off than I am now. As I am now, they may look as pious as they like—I laugh at them!"

And so forth: direr things. Imputations upon wives: horrible exultation at the universal peccancy of husbands. This lovely outcast almost made him think she had the right on her side, so keenly her Parthian arrows pierced the holy centres of society, and exposed its rottenness.

Mrs. Mount's house was discreetly conducted: nothing ever occurred to shock him there. The young man would ask himself where the difference was between her and the Women of society? How base, too, was the army of banded hypocrites! He was ready to declare war against them on her behalf. His casus beli, accurately worded, would have read curiously. Because the world refused to lure the lady to virtue with the offer of a housemaid's place, our knight threw down his challenge. But the lady had scornfully rebutted this prospect of a return to chastity. Then the form of the challenge must be: Because the world declined to support the lady in luxury for nothing! But what did that mean? In other words: she was to receive the devil's wages without rendering him her services. Such an arrangement appears hardly fair on the world or on the devil. Heroes will have to conquer both before they will get them to subscribe to it.

Heroes, however, are not in the habit of wording their declarations of war at all. Lance in rest they challenge and they charge. Like women they trust to instinct, and graft on it the muscle of men. Wide fly the leisurely-remonstrating hosts: institutions are scattered, they know not wherefore, heads are broken that have not the balm of a reason why. 'Tis instinct strikes! Surely there is something divine in instinct.

Still, war declared, where were these hosts? The hero could not charge down on the ladies and gentlemen in a ballroom, and spoil the quadrille. He had sufficient reticence to avoid sounding his challenge in the Law Courts; nor could he well go into the Houses of Parliament with a trumpet, though to come to a tussle with the nation's direct representatives did seem the likelier method. It was likewise out of the question that he should enter every house and shop, and battle with its master in the cause of Mrs. Mount. Where, then, was his enemy? Everybody was his enemy, and everybody was nowhere! Shall he convoke multitudes on Wimbledon Common? Blue Policemen, and a distant dread of ridicule, bar all his projects. Alas for the hero in our day!

Nothing teaches a strong arm its impotence so much as knocking at empty air.

"What can I do for this poor woman?" cried Richard, after fighting his phantom enemy till he was worn out.

"O Rip! old Rip!" he addressed his friend, "I'm distracted. I wish I was dead! What good am I for? Miserable! selfish! What have I done but make every soul I know wretched about me? I follow my own inclinations— I make people help me by lying as hard as they can—and I'm a liar. And when I've got it I'm ashamed of myself. And now when I do see something unselfish for me to do, I come upon grins—I don't know where to turn—how to act—and I laugh at myself like a devil!"

It was only friend Ripton's ear that was required, so his words went for little: but Ripton did say he thought there was small matter to be ashamed of in winning and wearing the Beauty of Earth. Richard added his customary comment of "Poor little thing!"

He fought his duello with empty air till he was exhausted. A last letter written to his father procured him no reply. Then, said he, I have tried my utmost. I have tried to be dutiful—my father won't listen to me. One thing I can do—I can go down to my dear girl, and make her happy, and save her at least from some of the consequences of my rashness.

"There's nothing better for me!" he groaned. His great ambition must be covered by a house-top: he and the cat must warm themselves on the domestic hearth! The hero was not aware that his heart moved him to this. His heart was not now in open communion with his mind.

Mrs. Mount heard that her friend was going—would go. She knew he was going to his wife. Far from discouraging him, she said nobly: "Go—I believe I have kept you. Let us have an evening together, and then go: for good, if you like. If not, then to meet again another time. Forget me. I shan't forget you. You're the best fellow I ever knew, Richard. You are, on my honour! I swear I would not step in between you and your wife to cause either of you a moment's unhappiness. When I can be another woman I will, and I shall think of you then."

Lady Blandish heard from Adrian that Richard was positively going to his wife. The wise youth modestly veiled his own merit in bringing it about by saying: "I couldn't see that poor little woman left alone down there any longer."

"Well! Yes!" said Mrs. Doria, to whom the modest speech was repeated, "I suppose, poor boy, it's the best he can do now."

Richard bade them adieu, and went to spend his last evening with Mrs. Mount.

The enchantress received him in state.

"Do you know this dress? No? It's the dress I wore when I first met you—not when I first saw you. I think I remarked you, sir, before you deigned to cast an eye upon humble me. When we first met we drank champagne together, and I intend to celebrate our parting in the same liquor. Will you liquor with me, old boy?"

She was gay. She revived Sir Julius occasionally. He, dispirited, left the talking all to her.

Mrs. Mount kept a footman. At a late hour the man of calves dressed the table for supper. It was a point of honour for Richard to sit down to it and try to eat. Drinking, thanks to the kindly mother nature, who loves to see her children made fools of, is always an easier matter. The footman was diligent; the champagne corks feebly recalled the file-firing at Richmond.

"We'll drink to what we might have been, Dick," said the enchantress.

Oh, the glorious wreck she looked.

His heart choked as he gulped the buzzing wine.

"What! down, my boy?" she cried. "They shall never see me hoist signals of distress. We must all die, and the secret of the thing is to die game, by Jove! Did you ever hear of Laura Fern? a superb girl! handsomer than your humble servant—if you'll believe it—a 'Miss' in the bargain, and as a consequence, I suppose, a much greater rake. She was in the hunting-field. Her horse threw her, and she fell plump on a stake. It went into her left breast. All the fellows crowded round her, and one young man, who was in love with her—he sits in the House of Peers now—we used to call him `Duck' because he was such a dear—he dropped from his horse to his knees: 'Laura! Laura! my darling! speak a word to me!—the last!' She turned over all white and bloody! 'I—I shan't be in at the death!' and gave up the ghost! Wasn't that dying game? Here's to the example of Laura Fenn! Why, what's the matter? See! it makes a man turn pale to hear how a woman can die. Fill the glasses, John. Why, you're as bad!"

"It's give me a turn, my lady," pleaded John, and the man's hand was unsteady as he poured out the wine.

"You ought not to listen. Go, and, drink some brandy."

John footman went from the room.

"My brave Dick! Richard! what a face you've got!"

He showed a deep frown on a colourless face.

"Can't you bear to hear of blood? You know, it was only one naughty woman out of the world. The clergyman of the parish didn't refuse to give her decent burial. We Christians! Hurrah!"

She cheered, and laughed. A lurid splendour glanced about her like lights from the pit.

"Pledge me, Dick! Drink, and recover yourself. Who minds? We must all die—the good and the bad. Ashes to ashes—dust to dust—and wine for living lips! That's poetry—almost. Sentiment: `May we never say die till we've drunk our fill! Not bad—eh? A little vulgar, perhaps, by Jove! Do you think me horrid?"

"Where's the wine?" Richard shouted. He drank a couple of glasses in succession, and stared about. Was he in hell, with a lost soul raving to him?

"Nobly spoken! and nobly acted upon, my brave Dick! Now we'll be companions." She wished that heaven had made her such a man. "Ah! Dick! Dick! too late! too late!"

Softly fell her voice. Her eyes threw slanting beams.

"Do you see this?"

She pointed to a symbolic golden anchor studded with gems and coiled with a rope of hair in her bosom. It was a gift of his.

"Do you know when I stole the lock? Foolish Dick! you gave me an anchor without a rope. Come and see."

She rose from the table, and threw herself on the sofa.

"Don't you recognize your own hair! I should know a thread of mine among a million."

Something of the strength of Samson went out of him as he inspected his hair on the bosom of Delilah.

"And you knew nothing of it! You hardly know it now you see it! What couldn't a woman steal from you? But you're not vain, and that's a protection. You're a miracle, Dick: a man that's not vain! Sit here." She curled up her feet to give him place on the sofa. "Now let us talk like friends that part to meet no more. You found a ship with fever on board, and you weren't afraid to come alongside and keep her company. The fever isn't catching, you see. Let us mingle our tears together. Ha! ha! a man said that once to me. The hypocrite wanted to catch the fever, but he was too old. How old are you, Dick?"

Richard pushed a few months forward.

> "Twenty-one? You just look it, you blooming boy. Now
> tell me my age,
> Adonis!—Twenty—what?"

Richard had given the lady twenty-five years.

She laughed violently. "You don't pay compliments, Dick. Best to be honest; guess again. You don't like to? Not twenty-five, or twenty- four, or twenty-three, or see how he begins to stare!—-twenty-two. Just twenty-one, my dear. I think my birthday's somewhere in next month. Why, look at me, close—closer. Have I a wrinkle?"

"And when, in heaven's name!"...he stopped short.

"I understand you. When did I commence for to live? At the ripe age of sixteen I saw a nobleman in despair because of my beauty. He vowed he'd die. I didn't want him to do that. So to save the poor man for his family, I ran away with him, and I dare say they didn't appreciate the sacrifice, and he soon forgot to, if he ever did. It's the way of the world!"

Richard seized some dead champagne, emptied the bottle into a tumbler, and drank it off.

John footman entered to clear the table, and they were left without further interruption.

"Bella! Bella!" Richard uttered in a deep sad voice, as he walked the room.

She leaned on her arm, her hair crushed against a reddened cheek, her eyes half-shut and dreamy.

"Bella!" he dropped beside her. "You are unhappy."

She blinked and yawned, as one who is awakened suddenly. "I think you spoke," said she.

"You are unhappy, Bella. You can't conceal it. Your laugh sounds like madness. You must be unhappy. So young, too! Only twenty-one!"

"What does it matter? Who cares for me?"

The mighty pity falling from his eyes took in her whole shape. She did not mistake it for tenderness, as another would have done.

"Who cares for you, Bella? I do. What makes my misery now, but to see you there, and know of no way of helping you? Father of mercy! it seems too much to have to stand by powerless while such ruin is going on!"

Her hand was shaken in his by the passion of torment with which his frame quaked.

Involuntarily a tear started between her eyelids. She glanced up at him quickly, then looked down, drew her hand from his, and smoothed it, eying it.

"Bella! you have a father alive!"

"A linendraper, dear. He wears a white neck-cloth."

This article of apparel instantaneously changed the tone of the conversation, for he, rising abruptly, nearly squashed the lady's lap- dog, whose squeaks and howls were piteous, and demanded the most fervent caresses of its mistress. It was: "Oh, my poor pet Mumpsy, and he didn't like a nasty great big ugly heavy foot an his poor soft silky—mum—mum—back, he didn't, and he soodn't that he—mum—mum—soodn't; and he cried out and knew the place to come to, and was oh so sorry for what had happened to him—mum—mum—mum—and now he was going to be made happy, his mistress make him happy—mum—mum—mum—moo-o-o-o."

"Yes!" said Richard, savagely, from the other end of the room, "you care for the happiness of your dog."

"A course se does," Mumpsy was simperingly assured in the thick of his silky flanks.

Richard looked for his hat. Mumpsy was deposited on the sofa in a twinkling.

"Now," said the lady, "you must come and beg Mumpsy's pardon, whether you meant to do it or no, because little doggies can't tell that—how should they? And there's poor Mumpsy thinking you're a great terrible rival that tries to squash him all flat to nothing, on purpose, pretending you didn't see; and he's trembling, poor dear wee pet! And I may love my dog, sir, if I like; and I do; and I won't have him ill-treated, for he's never been jealous of you, and he is a darling, ten times truer than men, and I love him fifty times better. So come to him with me."

First a smile changed Richard's face; then laughing a melancholy laugh, he surrendered to her humour, and went through the form of begging Mumpsy's pardon.

"The dear dog! I do believe he saw we were getting dull," said she.

"And immolated himself intentionally? Noble animal!"

"Well, we'll act as if we thought so. Let us be gay, Richard, and not part like ancient fogies. Where's your fun? You can rattle; why don't you? You haven't seen me in one of my characters—not Sir Julius: wait a couple of minutes." She ran out.

A white visage reappeared behind a spring of flame. Her black hair was scattered over her shoulders and fell half across her brows. She moved slowly, and came up to him, fastening weird eyes on him, pointing a finger at the region of witches. Sepulchral cadences accompanied the representation. He did not listen, for he was thinking what a deadly charming and exquisitely horrid witch she was. Something in the way her underlids worked seemed to remind him of a forgotten picture; but a veil hung on the picture. There could be no analogy, for this was beautiful and devilish, and that, if he remembered rightly, had the beauty of seraphs.

His reflections and her performance were stayed by a shriek. The spirits of wine had run over the plate she held to the floor. She had the coolness to put the plate down on the table, while he stamped out the flame on the carpet. Again she shrieked: she thought she was on fire. He fell on his knees and clasped her skirts all round, drawing his arms down them several times.

Still kneeling, he looked up, and asked, "Do you feel safe now?"

She bent her face glaring down till the ends of her hair touched his cheek.

Said she, "Do you?"

Was she a witch verily? There was sorcery in her breath; sorcery in her hair: the ends of it stung him like little snakes.

"How do I do it, Dick?" she flung back, laughing.

"Like you do everything, Bella," he said, and took breath.

"There! I won't be a witch; I won't be a witch: they may burn me to a cinder, but I won't be a witch!"

She sang, throwing her hair about, and stamping her feet.

"I suppose I look a figure. I must go and tidy myself."

"No, don't change. I like to see you so." He gazed at her with a mixture of wonder and admiration. "I can't think you the same person— not even when you laugh."

"Richard," her tone was serious, "you were going to speak to me of my parents."

"How wild and awful you looked, Bella!"

"My father, Richard, was a very respectable man."

"Bella, you'll haunt me like a ghost."

"My mother died in my infancy, Richard."

"Don't put up your hair, Bella."

"I was an only child!"

Her head shook sorrowfully at the glistening fire-irons. He followed the abstracted intentness of her look, and came upon her words.

"Ah, yes! speak of your father, Bella. Speak of him."

"Shall I haunt you, and come to your bedside, and cry, '`Tis time'?"

"Dear Bella! if you will tell me where he lives, I will go to him. He shall receive you. He shall not refuse—he shall forgive you."

"If I haunt you, you can't forget me, Richard."

"Let me go to your father, Bella let me go to him to-morrow. I'll give you my time. It's all I can give. O Bella! let me save you."

"So you like me best dishevelled, do you, you naughty boy! Ha! ha!" and away she burst from him, and up flew her hair, as she danced across the room, and fell at full length on the sofa.

He felt giddy: bewitched.

"We'll talk of everyday things, Dick," she called to him from the sofa. "It's our last evening. Our last? Heigho! It makes me sentimental. How's that Mr. Ripson, Pipson, Nipson?—it's not complimentary, but I can't remember names of that sort. Why do you have friends of that sort? He's not a gentleman. Better is he? Well, he's rather too insignificant for me. Why do you sit off there? Come to me instantly. There—I'll sit up, and be proper, and you'll have plenty of room. Talk, Dick!"

He was reflecting on the fact that her eyes were brown. They had a haughty sparkle when she pleased, and when she pleased a soft languor circled them. Excitement had dyed her cheeks deep red. He was a youth, and she an enchantress. He a hero; she a female will-o'-the-wisp.

The eyes were languid now, set in rosy colour.

"You will not leave me yet, Richard? not yet?"

He had no thought of departing:

"It's our last night—I suppose it's our last hour together in this world—and I don't want to meet you in the next, for poor Dick will have to come to such a very, very disagreeable place to make the visit."

He grasped her hand at this.

"Yes, he will! too true! can't be helped: they say I'm handsome."

"You're lovely, Bella."

She drank in his homage.

"Well, we'll admit it. His Highness below likes lovely women, I hear say. A gentleman of taste! You don't know all my accomplishments yet, Richard."

"I shan't be astonished at anything new, Bella."

"Then hear, and wonder." Her voice trolled out some lively roulades. "Don't you think he'll make me his prima donna below? It's nonsense to tell me there's no singing there. And the atmosphere will be favourable to the voice. No damp, you know. You saw the piano—why didn't you ask me to sing before? I can sing Italian. I had a master—who made love to me. I forgave him because of the music-stool—men can't help it on a music-stool, poor dears!"

She went to the piano, struck the notes, and sang—

"'My heart, my heart—I think 'twill break.'

"Because I'm such a rake. I don't know any other reason. No; I hate sentimental songs. Won't sing that. Ta-tiddy-tiddy-iddy—a...e! How ridiculous those women were, coming home from Richmond!

'Once the sweet romance of story
Clad thy moving form with grace;
Once the world and all its glory
Was but framework to thy face.
Ah, too fair!—what I remember
Might my soul recall—but no!
To the winds this wretched ember
Of a fire that falls so low!'

"Hum! don't much like that. Tum-te-tum-tum—accanto al fuoco—heigho! I don't want to show off, Dick—or to break down—so I won't try that.

'Oh! but for thee, oh! but for thee,
I might have been a happy wife,
And nursed a baby on my knee,
And never blushed to give it life.'

"I used to sing that when I was a girl, sweet Richard, and didn't know at all, at all, what it meant. Mustn't sing that sort of song in company. We're oh! so proper—even we!

'If I had a husband, what think you I'd do?
I'd make it my business to keep him a lover;
For when a young gentleman ceases to woo,
Some other amusement he'll quickly discover.'

"For such are young gentlemen made of—made of: such are young gentlemen made of!"

After this trifling she sang a Spanish ballad sweetly. He was in the mood when imagination intensely vivifies everything. Mere suggestions of music sufficed. The lady in the ballad had been wronged. Lo! it was the lady before him; and soft horns blew; he smelt the languid night-flowers; he saw the stars crowd large and close above the arid plain this lady leaning at her window desolate, pouring out her abandoned heart.

Heroes know little what they owe to champagne.

The lady wandered to Venice. Thither he followed her at a leap. In Venice she was not happy. He was prepared for the misery of any woman anywhere. But, oh! to be with her! To glide with phantom-motion through throbbing street; past houses muffled in shadow and gloomy legends; under storied bridges; past palaces charged with full life in dead quietness; past grand old towers, colossal squares, gleaming quays, and out, and on with her, on into the silver infinity shaking over seas!

Was it the champagne? the music? or the poetry? Something of the two former, perhaps: but most the enchantress playing upon him. How many instruments cannot clever women play upon at the same moment! And this enchantress was not too clever, or he might have felt her touch. She was no longer absolutely bent on winning him, or he might have seen a manoeuvre. She liked him—liked none better. She wished him well. Her pique was satisfied. Still he was handsome, and he was going. What she liked him for, she rather—very slightly—wished to do away with, or see if it could be done away with: just as one wishes to catch a pretty butterfly, without hurting its patterned wings. No harm intended to the innocent insect, only one wants to inspect it thoroughly, and enjoy the marvel of it, in one's tender possession, and have the felicity of thinking one could crush it, if one would.

He knew her what she was, this lady. In Seville, or in Venice, the spot was on her. Sailing the pathways of the moon it was not celestial light that illumined her beauty. Her sin was there: but in dreaming to save, he was soft to her sin—drowned it in deep mournfulness.

Silence, and the rustle of her dress, awoke him from his musing. She swam wave-like to the sofa. She was at his feet.

> "I have been light and careless to-night, Richard. Of
> course I meant it.
> I must be happy with my best friend going to leave me."

Those witch underlids were working brightly.

"You will not forget me? and I shall try…try…"

Her lips twitched. She thought him such a very handsome fellow.

"If I change—if I can change… Oh! if you could know what a net I'm in, Richard!"

Now at those words, as he looked down on her haggard loveliness, not divine sorrow but a devouring jealousy sprang like fire in his breast, and set him rocking with horrid pain. He bent closer to her pale beseeching face. Her eyes still drew him down.

"Bella! No! no! promise me! swear it!"

"Lost, Richard! lost for ever! give me up!"

He cried: "I never will!" and strained her in his arms, and kissed her passionately on the lips.

She was not acting now as she sidled and slunk her half-averted head with a kind of maiden shame under his arm, sighing heavily, weeping, clinging to him. It was wicked truth.

Not a word of love between them!

Was ever hero in this fashion won?